EVEN CRAZIER

CRAZY ELLA IN LOVE : 2

EVE LANGLAIS

Even Crazier Copyright © 2018, Eve Langlais

Cover Art © 2018 Dreams2media

Produced in Canada

Published by Eve Langlais

www.EveLanglais.com

ALL RIGHTS RESERVED

This Book is a work of fiction and the characters, events and dialogue found within the story are of the author's imagination and are not to be construed as real. Any resemblance to actual events or persons, either living or deceased, is completely coincidental.

No part of this book may be reproduced or shared in any form or by any means, electronic or mechanical, including but not limited to digital copying, file sharing, audio recording, email and printing without permission in writing from the author.

eBook ISBN: 978-1-77384-0567

Print ISBN: 978-1-77384-0574

PROLOGUE

FELICIA AWOKE IN DARKNESS, the candle long snuffed out. The creep of dawn had yet to lighten her window, and yet her eyes remained open, sleep having fled.

Something roused her.

A stir in the shadows halted her breath, and she clutched her blanket to her chest. "Who's there?" Who dared invade her bedchamber at night? And how?

The bar across the door was a sturdy precaution her mother insisted on when Father and his soldiers returned loud and lusty from battle. There was no entrance to her room but the window, several stories above ground. Only a bird could manage to enter. Yet she didn't think it was a mere animal in her room. She felt eyes watching.

Don't be afraid. The words whispered across her skin. *Relax.*

"I will not relax," she huffed. "Who are you?

Show yourself." She refused to show fear even if inside she trembled. Never show weakness. How often did she hear Father bark those very same words?

"You are an impertinent chit." The harshness of the statement created a chill that pimpled her skin. From the shadows by her wardrobe emerged a figure. His raiments were rich, the fabric thick and woven of many colors. Garish and better suited for court with the king than invading a young lady's bedroom at night.

"How dare you come in here? My father will kill you." Because now that she'd reached marriageable age, she held much value.

"Your father will never know. Because you aren't going to tell. You're not going to say a word at all. Bare your neck to me."

The words hit her, and she blinked. Wanted to laugh at his demand and then scream for her father's guards. They'd eviscerate this stranger.

Yet...she found her lips sealed. She let go of the sheet she held for modesty, and it fell to her lap. She tilted her head and bared her throat. Only fluttered her lashes once when the fangs slid into her skin.

Good thing she'd bathed. She'd hate to think that the stranger in her room sucked on a dirty neck.

Shouldn't I be screaming? There is someone drinking my blood.

And it felt good. The trepidation she'd felt vanished at the pleasure. A smile pulled at her lips, and she uttered a contented sigh. Maybe she'd cry for help later.

Instead, she fell asleep and thought the whole thing a dream until she saw the bruise on her neck the next day.

She covered it. Obviously, some kind of bug had gotten to her. The idea there was a stranger in her rooms...absurd.

That night she shook her sheets. Crushed sprigs of mint in every corner. Then, as a precaution, she double-checked her door was barred and ensured the window was shut as well.

'Twas but a dream.

Wrong.

The vampire returned. He came for three nights in a row and feasted on her flesh. Whispered things he'd do to her. Vile stuff.

A precursor to events still to come. Because, after that first night, he didn't just drink her blood. He made her act in a way that shamed her. Dirty ways her mother would have called a sin.

He should have picked someone else.

On the fourth night, Felicia had her father's favorite hunting knife tucked under her pillow. The vampire—who wasn't legend after all—appeared more surprised than angry when she shoved it into his heart and twisted.

His mouth opened and closed. Blood bubbled at his lips. She struggled beneath him as his body pinned hers, and he gave her a final deadly kiss, slick and coppery with blood, as his hands strangled her to death.

Oh dear.

Except she didn't really die.

The next night, she woke on her funeral bed...hungry.

No survivors were found when the fire in the castle finally burned itself out.

ONE

HUNGER PROVED a gnawing distraction as the lesson came to a close. The beating pulse distracted. All that lovely pumping blood. Felicia did wonder at the flavor.

Sweet or tart?

A pity she'd never know. Zane would kill her if she took a bite. He might still murder Felicia if she didn't find a way to help the woman he'd taken as mate.

"Concentrate, Ella," Felicia told a petite woman whose fragile features were framed by a blonde skein of hair that hung past her shoulders. It held natural highlights of platinum and shimmered as she shook her head in agitation.

"I am concentrating," grumped Ella. She was about as angry looking as a baby squirrel.

"If you were actually paying attention and trying, then I wouldn't have to tell you because we'd see a result. Focus your power." Strange role for Felicia.

Teacher for a power she'd never encountered before. An ánima veneficus, a sorceress who could manipulate ghosts.

Ella's nose wrinkled, and her fists clenched—as cute as a kitten getting annoyed. "You know I can't just turn it on at will."

Or so Ella thought. Felicia knew better. She had quickly grasped upon their first meeting that the young woman was capable of powerful magic if she damned well tried. "You can access it, so stop pretending otherwise."

"Only when I'm stressed."

"Being able to act only in times of emotional distress is not good enough."

"I'm fine with it."

"You shouldn't be!" Felicia snapped. "You should aspire to more than mediocrity."

"I'm just fine being simple old me." The worst part? Ella meant it.

"Ever think you're supposed to do more than just hang around Zane's house eating ice cream?"

"Nothing wrong with chillaxing." Ella beamed. Since she'd escaped the asylum—where she'd spent most of her life after her parents had her committed for hearing voices—she'd spent a lot of time trying to absorb today's culture and slang. Every time they met, Ella threw a new one at Felicia.

"You can't be a lazy bum forever. What if you need to help someone? Like Zane."

"Why would Zane need help?" Ella laughed. "He's tough enough already."

Indeed, Zane, an old friend and ally, could very well take care of things on his own. He didn't hesitate when it came to protecting what he was. But... "What if humans attack en masse during the day? You going to let him die because you're being silly about using your skills?"

"No."

"Then learn to use your gifts." Felicia pointed to an ornate chair, her throne of several hundred pounds. "Lift it."

Ella cast it a glance and didn't mock it like Zane would. The damned man called it garish. Whereas Felicia rather thought the rose-gold sheathing gave it a certain cachet, as did the etchings of twining, thorny vines ending in roses where, if you looked carefully, you could see the screaming faces of the enemies she'd vanquished.

Good memories. A reminder of how hard she'd fought to get where she was. Top of the food chain. No one could touch her. No one dared disobey, except Ella.

The young woman pointed to the throne. "I can't lift that. It is way too heavy."

"Weight is immaterial." Felicia waved dismissively, the manicure on her fingers perfect. French, of course, with rounded white tips. "The forces you command are beyond such things as weight or size."

"Says you. You're not the one doing the lifting."

"And neither are you. The ghosts are the ones actually accomplishing the task." While most of the time they couldn't affect much in the real world, something about their proximity with Ella allowed them to move things. An awesome power. A good thing it hadn't fallen into the wrong hands. She'd hate to kill the girl.

"My friends in the attic aren't being too cooperative at the moment."

"That is because you are too nice." Felicia's lip curled. Everything about Ella was nice, which made Zane's capitulation all the more incredible. Once the most bloodthirsty of all the vampires in her court, Zane now smiled and did thoughtful things like bring his mate fresh bouquets of flowers and ice cream sundaes with extra cherries. The travesty! Didn't he remember the first rule?

Don't date your food.

But he'd not just dated it; he married it. It boggled the mind how this tiny woman, with the innocent airs, snared the most eligible vampire bachelor. How?

Seriously, Felicia wanted to know. A part of her envied the happiness they'd found.

Craved it even more than fresh blood.

How long had it been since she'd even given a man a second glance? It didn't help the males she met found her intimidating. She could never hope to pull off an innocent act. Centuries of vice had jaded her.

"Nothing wrong with being nice," Ella claimed.

"Except for the fact it makes no sense. Of all the people I know, you have one of the best reasons for hating everyone and wanting revenge." Ella had been institutionalized at a young age for hearing voices. Felicia didn't need to know particulars to understand the trauma this inflicted. Yet, Ella, with a sweet smile, never let anything get her down. She saw the positive in everything. The glass half full.

Blech. Felicia considered herself a realist, and the only person she trusted was herself. With good reason. Those most likely to betray were the ones closest to you. They only ever did it once. She dealt with perfidy immediately and harshly. This vampire queen hadn't managed to maintain her reign by being *nice*.

Ella, however, just didn't understand. She made excuses for bad behavior. "Hate solves nothing. Most times people are just confused. Once you explain things properly..." She smiled.

"I find explaining things with knives works best." Many shallow slices, enough to hurt and bleed but keep the subject alive a long time. To ensure they learned their lesson.

"Violence isn't the answer. Love is."

Before Felicia could slap sense into Ella, the blonde canted her head, and her brow creased as if she listened to someone.

"Don't you interrupt me, Brenda." Ella shook a finger at a blank spot in front of her. "Just because you're still angry at Harold for sleeping with Mary-Sue at your funeral is no reason to get aggressive. I was talking to my friend."

What a concept. A vampire queen friends with a

human sorceress. Even odder, it brought a not often felt warmth to Felicia's breast. She fought it. "What have I said about using the f-word?"

But Ella ignored her, still intent on the blank spot in front of her. Apparently, Brenda had a reply because Ella crossed her arms and got a stubborn expression. Not the mulish kind, more a baby goat.

"Go ahead and try, Brenda." Ella beckoned with her fingers. "You wanna take me? I dare you. But be warned, I might not know how to do many things, but I do know how to send a ghost away on a long trip."

A recent skill Ella had learned when a few of the more aggressive spirits began harassing her to find their families. They wouldn't take no for an answer and haunted Ella day and night. Which apparently cut into her time with Zane. The one thing Ella wasn't nice about.

But disrupting her boudoir time with her lover wasn't the only reason Ella snapped and sent the ghosts away. Ella drew the line at passing on instructions from the dead. According to her, the dead should never dictate to the living. Some kind of cardinal rule.

However, those ghosts refused to listen. They got loud and violent when they didn't get their way. Zane later told Felicia that the poltergeists, in a tantrum, ripped books from the library shelves and began flying them in a maelstrom around Ella. When she still wouldn't comply, they began tossing those books at Zane. That caused Ella to get angry enough to lash out.

When things calmed, the three worst ghosts were gone. Never to be heard from since.

Things got much calmer around Ella after that as the remaining ghosts behaved.

But new ghosts were created daily, which meant those who'd not seen the lesson began the harassment anew. How long before Ella lost her temper again?

Soon, Felicia hoped. She'd like to see Miss Perfect act normal for once.

Ella continued her conversation with her invisible harasser. "You know what, Brenda? I think you should go on a trip. Make new friends. Guy friends. You are, after all, a widow now."

The oddity of calling a ghost a widow struck Felicia. But then again, it did fit. Brenda didn't have a husband at the moment. All bonds severed at death.

"Yes, you are single. Which means you can date." Ella grinned, still at a blank spot in the air. "You could totally rock a bikini. I hear the Bermuda Triangle is particularly strong with those living the afterlife this time of year."

Felicia cleared her throat. "If you're done playing travel agent to a spirit, can we get on with the lesson?"

Uncanny eyes met hers, the depths of them swirling with a white/gray mist. "We'll finish practice another time. I want to hear about the genies before I go home."

In the midst of pouring a few fingers of infused brandy—the infusion being some of the proteins found in blood, vampire vitamins so to speak; it drastically cut down her need to feed—Felicia didn't pause. She filled the amber liquid to the midway point in the crystal glass. She clutched it with two fingers and a thumb before idly turning. "Excuse me? What are you talking about?"

"The genies coming to visit you."

"I haven't the slightest idea of what you speak."

Ella snorted. "You know you can't lie to me. Some of my friends up here"—she tapped her temple—"told me that there are genies coming to visit you. I can't believe you didn't tell me. That is so freaking cool."

"First off, they are djinn, and you would do well to use that rather than the slang made popular by cartoons and film."

"Whatever. When are they arriving?"

Felicia's turn to cross her arms. "You want information, then you need to give me something first. Lift it." She angled her head at the chair.

"Seriously? Blackmail?"

"Negotiation."

"Fine." Ella sighed. She pinched her features, and her frame went stiff. The throne lifted a half-inch, shifted over a few, and dropped. Ella opened her eyes and smiled. "I did it. Now it's my turn to get something. I want to meet one."

Without hesitation. "No."

"Why not?"

"Because their visit is supposed to be a secret." A matter of grave import the message said before it self-destructed. Intriguing and old-fashioned given it arrived by owl, tied to its leg in a small vial that tingled when she touched it. The tiny scrap of paper appeared as gibberish at first, but then words appeared. A note warning the djinn were coming. Giving her the option of saying no.

As if she'd refuse. She wanted to meet the reclusive race.

"I won't tell anyone. Just invite me to dinner. Tell them I'm your assistant or cousin or something."

"No."

"You are such a spoilsport. Can you at least tell me their names, maybe hook me up with their Instagram and Twitter profiles so I can stalk them online?"

The reference to social media had her blinking. "Did Zane seriously think allowing you Internet access was a good idea?"

"Zane encourages my learning."

"The only thing you'll learn via social media and other online sources is flashy headlines based on little substance. It is a fake world." Which she refused to join. Bad enough her cell phone made her accessible at all hours of the day. She missed when carrier birds or messengers on fast horses had to take days, sometimes weeks, to travel. It was a slower pace of life then.

"Some of it is fake, but if you know where to look, you can learn a lot. About regular stuff anyhow. Other things are a bit harder to figure out. Such as, does a genie dude live in a lamp or a bottle?"

"You cannot ask that." Nor did Felicia plan to, even if she wondered herself. Legend had vampires sleeping in coffins. Which was false. She slept in a bed, with good drapes. At her age, direct sunlight wouldn't kill on contact, but it would sizzle and leave her looking like a lobster dropped in boiling water.

"How am I supposed to learn about the genies and their culture if I can't ask questions?"

"You won't ask questions because you're not meeting them."

"Yes I am." Stated with a quiet assurance that Felicia knew wouldn't waver. If Ella said it would happen, then it would.

"You want to know about the djinn? Then, for starters, how about we don't treat them like they're different. They're people just like you and me." For hundreds of years, Felicia had been teaching people that vampires could coexist with humans and not eat everyone they met.

Hundreds. Of. Years.

The lesson still hadn't stuck. Humans learned and then died of old age, meaning new ones had to be taught to take their place. Then there were the unfortunate incidents where vampires actually did snack on unsuspecting humans.

Image tarnished.

And she was tired of fixing it.

"But we *are* different," Ella retorted. "Which is okay. It's what makes the world an interesting place."

Felicia resisted an urge to rub her forehead. "Being different isn't the problem. It's the incessant badgering questions that are the issue. Why can't you simply listen?"

"How come it's okay for you to ask me about my magic and my childhood and how long my periods last, but I can't ask some guy if Aladdin was real?"

A smile lurked around the corners of Felicia's lips. "Aladdin was very real. He belonged to a political party that fell out of favor about eight centuries ago. So tread carefully before mentioning his name."

Ella's mouth rounded. "Oh. That's fascinating."

"I have a book about it in the library if you'd like to borrow it."

"I just might, and then maybe I can find a ghost still around from that time." The world relied on Google and translations of recovered texts for history. Ella spoke to those who lived it.

Major envy moment.

"Asking a ghost is a better idea than asking a djinn," Felicia remarked.

"If gin is for one, is it ginnie or gins for two or more?"

"Still djinn."

"What do they look like?"

"Whatever they want. Puff of smoke. Dragon. Man. Woman. I once knew one that chose to be a four-foot blue-skinned troll." Poor Baku. He ended up being eaten by a goblin who thought he was a new flavor.

"You've had a zillion adventures and met a ton of people. You're so lucky."

Lucky? Not quite the word Felicia used. The term

survivor came to mind. There were a few moments in her past she'd rather erase. "Adventure is not as glamorous as you'd think." For one thing, it usually involved sleeping in cramped, dirty holes hidden from daylight and people bearing wooden stakes. And I should add that if you chose to spend less time watching Netflix—"

"And chilling with my man!"

"—you could see more of the world."

"I'll be seeing it soon enough. The time of portent arrives with quickening steps," Ella said with utmost seriousness. Before Felicia could question the odd statement, Ella clapped her hands. "What time do they arrive tomorrow?"

Was there any point in hiding it? "Seven p.m. And it's tonight." Just over sixteen hours away.

"Why aren't you preparing?"

A snort escaped Felicia. "You do know I have staff for that kind of stuff."

"Don't you have to shop for a slinky dress? What if they're cute?"

"No need to shop. I have a closetful of garments." Something to suit every occasion, including rarely used items of seduction. It had been so long since she'd worn that finery it would probably disintegrate into dust if touched.

The distant purr of an engine drew her attention. Felicia tipped back the rest of her glass before saying, "We are done for today. I hear Zane arriving." She heard just about everything that happened in her house. Spells placed by warlocks and elven mages amplified the sound in the rooms she wanted to spy on. Nothing happened that she wasn't aware of.

Ella whirled and faced the door, eager as always to greet her lover. She wasn't alone in her haste. Zane walked with purposeful energy whenever he came to fetch Ella. And he never failed to show. Ella never traveled alone. He displayed a protectiveness that bordered on claustrophobic, at least for Felicia. But Ella didn't mind it. A good thing because ever since Zane had paid a visit to the woman who'd placed Ella in the asylum, he'd been tense. Apparently, Ella's past held some secrets. Zane said something about a prophecy, which Felicia didn't pay much mind. Prophecies that were given too much attention had a tendency of being self-fulfilling.

However, Zane was worried. He was the one who insisted Felicia work Ella hard. He never said it, but Felicia got the impression he was concerned an untrained Ella might actually become a menace to the world. One could only hope. Felicia found the concept intriguing enough to overlook Ella's cheerful nature.

"Zane!" Sunshine and happiness. That was the expression on Ella's face each time Zane walked into a room.

It was revolting. Clingy.

Adorable. Enviable.

Felicia turned away from the embrace. "Get a room."

"Or you could just leave. We've not yet done it on a throne," was the deep baritone reply.

The very idea had her glaring at Zane, who stared at her with a mocking grin, his arms looped loosely around Ella.

"Don't you dare," Felicia stated.

"Now you know I will."

Felicia flung her hands. "Bah, the pair of you drive me insane. You, with your teenage libido and her, with her laziness."

"I am not lazy," Ella hotly retorted. "I'm not taking advantage of my attic friends just because your throne's not centered."

Felicia's gaze narrowed. How did she know? Was it really that noticeable? "Fine, you're not lazy, but you do lack proper control."

"I controlled it just fine when I had to."

The problem with vanquishing a badass, say like the recently defeated sorcerer who tried to use Ella's power, was the false self-assurance. "A fluke. What if next time you're up against someone with more skill?"

"I can handle trouble."

"The correct answer is to eliminate trouble." How many times did she have to say it?

"And there's the problem," Ella said to Zane. "Why must I always kill? Why can't I just give someone a firm scare? A second chance?"

Zane tugged his shirt up and showed off a rather ridged scar. Left by a feral vampire, the enzymes in the bite meant the flesh never fully healed. "This is what happens when you allow the wrong person a second chance."

Ella ran her fingers over it. "I thought you said a bad vampire did this."

"A bad vampire I had the opportunity to stop." He dropped the shirt. "Sometimes showing mercy is the wrong thing to do."

"Your reluctance to act is a danger not only to yourself but others," Felicia added.

An eye roll accompanied Ella's sigh. "If I have to kill, I'll kill." The chilling words lost their punch spoken in her sweet voice.

Felicia snorted. "Can't you make it sound at least a little ominous?"

"You want ominous?" The deep voice emerged from a suddenly rigid Ella. "He who rides is coming. He who craves is hungering. He who died is living. He who bows survives."

It obviously wasn't Ella speaking. "Who are you?" Felicia snapped.

Meanwhile, poor Zane looked frantic as he didn't know who to fight. Ella was in danger; anyone could see it by the red glow emanating from her eyes. "Get out of my wife!" he shouted, fists clenched, a vein in his temple throbbing.

"I am he who comes. The destroyer of nations. Leader of the legions." The red spark in her eyes flared brighter, and Ella's hair lifted in a staticky halo.

"What do you want?" Zane growled. "Leave my wife alone."

"She will serve me," the thing inside Ella hissed. "All will bow. All will serve. All—"

Felicia had heard enough.

Crack. Her hand connected with Ella's cheek. She snapped, "Fight. Take back control."

"She can't because she is mine." The voice laughed.

Felicia didn't let it chill her as intended. She knew of a way to grab Ella's attention. She flung herself at Zane and wrapped her arms around him.

Zane, who'd stiffened on contact, grasped her idea. He smiled down at Felicia, or his lips did at least. His eyes remained stone cold.

"Aaaaaaaaarhhhhr." The sound whistled out of Ella's mouth as her head thrashed from side to side.

Ran a finger down his cheek.

Ella snapped. She yelled, "Out!" and her arms flung away from her body, sending out a wave of scorching air that whipped past Felicia's skin, smelling of the desert sands. Then, as quickly as it hit, it was gone, leaving behind a deep silence broken by Ella declaring, "Well, that was unexpected."

TWO

"IT ONLY POSSESSED ME FOR A MINUTE," Ella explained for the zillionth time as they drove home. She tried to downplay it.

Zane still freaked. "What do you mean it possessed you? How does that happen, Ella? I thought you controlled the spirits."

"I do, but like I told you back at Felicia's place, whatever took over was more than a spirit." The presence that stepped into her body and wore her like a suit glowed with the heat of a hundred suns. Filled her to almost bursting. He didn't spark in her presence like a regular ghost; he exploded.

"Saying it was more than a spirit doesn't reassure me, moonbeam."

"It's not as if I got hurt. He only wanted to relay a message."

"About the apocalypse coming." Zane's hands gripped the wheel tight.

"That seems a rather dark analysis for the poem."

"How else can you interpret it?" He took his eyes off the road long enough to ask.

"How bad can it be? It did say 'dead to alive.' Someone's getting a second chance. Good for them."

Zane gaped at her. "I don't believe you just fucking said that." He turned his head to stare at the road once more, his jaw a grim line of annoyance.

It took biting her lip to hold in a snicker. Sometimes baiting her husband was just too easy. But Ella had to do it. Had to lighten the mood because she couldn't let Zane know how terrified she was. Shaking inside her own skin.

Which was better than being shoved out of it.

Having never experienced it before, it took her by surprise when the evil spirit hijacked her body, leaving Ella in a strange limbo, watching herself.

I really need to do something about my bangs. And that ugly pair of pants. They made her look like she had no butt.

It took her a moment to register what had happened. To realize her body had been kidnapped. A second longer before she acted. Ghost Ella flew at the thing occupying her body and slammed at it. Might as well hit a wall. It kept her out, didn't even waver.

When Felicia slapped her, she didn't even feel it. But seeing the queen, with her curvy frame, drape herself on Zane, touching her husband... Jealousy made her scream, and the noise snapped the ghosts out of their shock. Together they rushed Ella's body and shoved out the fiend wearing it.

Or did he relinquish it because he'd imparted his message? Either way, she snapped back into herself. Terrified, but unable to show it. Worried, because if it happened once, it could happen again.

Worse, what if the ghosts decided to try the same trick? A few she could hold off, but what if they banded? What if they saw her weakness? What if... What if...

Imagining Felicia, she gave herself a mental slap. *I am stronger than this*. Ella didn't crack in the asylum. She wasn't cracking now, and part of the reason why she wouldn't was sitting beside her.

Zane. Her husband. Her lover. Her rock.

She leaned against his arm, the close interior of his sports car making it easy to snuggle. She put a hand on his thigh. "Don't worry about me. I'm fine."

"You'd better be."

"It didn't hurt."

"You weren't in control."

"I beat it," she lied. Maybe.

"You got lucky, dammit." She heard a crack as he fisted the steering wheel a tad too tight. He loved her so much.

And she loved him. So much at times it scared her. The only thing she feared was losing him, a fear she knew he suffered from, too. But if there was something she'd learned since she met him, it was that the sex was always best after the danger was past.

Her hand moved from his thigh to the spot between them. She rubbed the bulge there. It grew with every stroke.

"E-l-l-a." He stretched her name.

"Yes?" She smiled and cupped him before letting her fingers work at his zipper.

"I'm driving."

"Pay attention, then." Her head dropped into his lap, her warm breath blowing on the erection she freed from his pants. "So, tell me, husband." She purred the word onto his cock. "How come you haven't taught me to drive yet? I could totally handle a stick." She wrapped her fingers around him.

A raspy quality invaded his reply. "Maybe you should show me."

She blew hotly across the tip of cock and felt him shudder. She treasured intimate moments like these, just the two of them, no ghosts. They didn't like Zane and shut right up when she touched him.

She touched him a lot.

She also liked to taste him. In her mouth. Sucking on him while he drove, hearing him curse she'd kill them both, was one of the highlights of her day. Especially when he slammed the car onto a shoulder of road, rammed his seat as far back as it would go, and dragged her onto his lap, facing away from him.

"I wasn't done," she protested.

"Don't worry. I'll help you finish." His hands tugged at her pants, baring her bottom. The rigid length of him poked, and she held on to the steering wheel to balance herself as he lifted her enough he could guide himself into her.

The thickness of him stretched her, and she sighed with pleasure as she sank down. His hands gripped her around the waist, helping her to rock and grind against him, driving him deep. Bringing her the pleasure she craved.

"Zane." She whispered his name and he replied by sliding a hand between her thighs to play with her clitoris, rubbing it as he thrust into her. Faster and faster. Pleasure—that glorious, body-shuddering ecstasy he always gave—rolled through her. Shook her. Shook him.

For a moment after, they remained joined.

"Have I told you how much I love car sex?" she finally said.

"One of these days, moonbeam, your need for it is going to get one of us hurt."

"Don't be a grump." She squirmed atop him, and he groaned.

The frosted windows meant they didn't see who knocked, but it did startle.

Ella rolled off Zane's lap and wriggled her pants back over her girly parts while Zane just had to zip.

"I swear, if we get another ticket because you can't keep it in your pants," she said with a giggle.

"Another for the collection." He grinned at Ella and winked as he rolled down the window. Not paying attention. Never seeing the gun aimed at his head.

Ella screamed as the weapon went off.

THREE

THE KNOCK CAME at the ungodly hour of seven a.m. A knock Felicia shouldn't have heard, yet for some reason, it sounded freakishly loud.

She hid under her pillow rather than answer. She'd learned in the fourteenth century to ignore knocks before noon. And after noon. Anything before dusk or after dawn just wasn't conducive to a vampire's continued good health.

The knock came again. A rapid pounding.

Seriously? Rolling onto her back, she shoved the pillow over her head and added fingers to her ears.

Still not answering. Either the knocker would get the point, or one of her lazy staff would answer despite her orders. She'd fire them if they did. Six to six. The rules were very clear. No visitors. Not even deliveries. Which begged the question, how did the person even get onto the grounds? They should have never made it past the guarded gate. And what of her personal guards? They roamed the grounds. They protected the house. They should have shot the knocker's ass before he even made it up the steps!

The third knock was a single fierce boom. The entire house shook, and more than ever, she wouldn't answer. Nothing good would come of it.

The reverberations died, and no other knocks occurred. She relaxed. Removed the pillow from her head. Sighed as she snuggled into the bed she'd crawled into at five a.m., less than two hours ago.

Then screamed as a voice said, "Boo!"

Jumping to her feet, Felicia hollered, "Lights," and reached into the canopy that ringed her bed for the rapier she kept stashed. It had been awhile since she'd had to pull the steel blade; however, like other things that never changed, every few years, someone tried to accost her while she slept. She blamed those *Dusk 'til Dawn* movies. They made vampire killing seem cool. What they failed to properly portray was it never ended well—for the humans.

Vampires were top of the food chain and ruthless about staying there. The hilt of the sword filled her hand, and she twirled with it, jabbing in the direction of...nothing.

"Missed me." The taunt came from her left.

Whirl and stab.

"Missed me again."

This time from her right. Another lunge and miss.

A fast foe. Making a mockery of her. She closed her eyes rather than look for someone she couldn't see.

She let her other senses take over.

Heard his teasing whisper at her ear. "Hello, beautiful."

She ignored the words and shot her hand straight forward. Made contact. Only when she gripped someone by the neck did she open her eyes.

The lamps that lit at her command meant she could see she held a man. A tall man. She stood on her plush bed, and he still managed to look her in the eyes. The height of her bed plus her five-foot-two had to make him close to eight feet. Impossible.

She looked down. Noticed his feet didn't touch the floor. He levitated, and yet she wouldn't let that intimidate her. She held the upper hand since she literally had him by the throat. "Who are you?" Other than delicious looking.

The stranger had a deep tan to his skin, the kind she'd wager didn't come from baking in the sun. His complexion went well with his dark hair and short, pointed beard. He wore a jewel-toned button shirt, slightly open at the neck. It clung to broad shoulders. A lovely hint of cinnamon spiced his scent. It didn't take her seeing the flashing spark of green in his eyes to guess who she'd caught. But she still asked. "Who are you? How did you get in here?"

He answered only the first question. "I am Tariq." No last name, no need of one, given his kind were almost extinct. "And you are the vampire queen. Felicia Dupuy. We meet at last."

"Speaking of meeting, you're early. I wasn't expecting you and the other djinn until tonight."

"We agreed on seven."

"P.M."

"Was it?" A hint of a smirk hovered around his lips.

He darned well knew it was seven p.m. yet thought he could play games. "I assume it was you pounding at this ungodly hour."

"Ungodly only to believers in those deities. Personally, I tend to worship myself." He winked, long, thick lashes over intense eyes.

How dare he be wickedly delicious looking? The scent of him entranced. Her mouth watered. How long since her last Persian meal? Judging by the interest stirring in her body, too long

"How did you get past the defense wards?"

"You had wards?" He blinked, but he totally missed looking innocent. On the contrary, the wickedness in his gaze lit the spot between her legs.

She fought his allure. "Yes, I had wards. Damn it. The warlock who sold them to me swore they'd work."

He smiled. "I'd ask for my money back."

"I will." With blood interest.

"Were you planning to massage my neck all day?" he asked.

She looked at her hand, small and contrasting against his thick neck. She squeezed a little tighter and angled the sword she still held so that the tip pointed at his face. "You broke into my house and invaded my bedchamber."

"I broke nothing." His lip curled with mischief. "But I can't deny I am in your room."

"Why?"

"Because you're in it. How else was I supposed to meet you?"

"By showing up at your appointed time."

His smile widened. "Where's the fun in that?"

"Where are your companions?" The note had implied there would be more than one seeking her audience. A group of djinn. The mysteries she could unravel with one visit. Not much was known about the reclusive race. They kept to themselves. She couldn't recall the last time she'd heard of one making an appearance.

"They'll be along later today. They stuck to more conventional methods of travel."

"You should follow their example." She finally released him and tucked her hand behind her back. Because now that she had touched his skin, she wanted to keep on touching. No one had warned her a djinn would ooze sex appeal.

He drifted down until his feet touched the ground and took a step away from the bed, but only so he could better appraise her, it appeared. His gaze raked her head to foot, taking in every inch.

Let him. He wouldn't see much. Harkening to a simpler past, she wore a white cotton gown. Neck to ankle, nothing revealing about it.

"Sexy," he growled.

"You've been in your bottle too long," was her quick retort. How would he react to the insult?

The corners of his eyes crinkled, and he laughed. "Quick-witted as well as beautiful."

"And you're a flirt. Judging by the request I received, I assumed our meeting would be serious."

"It is very serious. Life and death, you might even say."

"Is that a threat?"

"Not to you. I come to you as a supplicant in need of aid." Said by a man who held himself tall and arrogant.

"Or you're pulling a Trojan horse."

"What reason would I have to go to war with the vampires?"

"You tell me. You are the one who messaged me out of the blue. Who asked for sanctuary." An ancient request she'd not heard in centuries.

His gaze darkened. "I wouldn't have asked if the need wasn't great."

"Why?"

"Such impatience. You'll find out soon when I arrive with my companions."

"Arrive? But you're already here."

"I can't stay. I must return to my travel mates. But first, a kiss for luck."

"Excuse me? I don't—"

The firm press of his lips against hers happened before she finished the sentence. How he'd gone from a few feet away to face to face, she didn't know. But she felt it.

Felt the firm press of his mouth on hers. A tingling started in more than one place on her body. Before she could think to slap him for his impunity, he disappeared in a swirl of bluish-gray smoke.

What the hell just happened? She pressed her fingers to her lips.

Had she dreamt the whole thing? Felicia appeared to be wide-awake, but to make sure, she rewound the video footage for her room. Watched the whole thing from his sudden appearance—the kiss—to his departure.

It really did happen. She'd met her first djinn. Kissed her first djinn. Perhaps the next time she saw him, she'd feast on her first djinn. The nerve of him, treating her like a common trollop.

She couldn't remember the last time that happened. The last time a kiss managed to wet her cleft…

Since sleep appeared determined to evade her, she wrapped a robe around herself and went to her home office. A flashing light caught her attention. Her cell phone beckoned from its charging stand.

A message at this stupidly early hour. Never a good sign.

She dialed into the voicemail and listened.

"Felicia." Ella's panicked voice came through the line. Her breathing frantic. "Oh my God. Where are you? I need you. Someone shot Zane!"

What? Felicia froze as she listened.

"He's okay," Ella rushed on to add, "but the person who shot us isn't. Zane ate him."

Probably to replenish what he'd lost. Not a surprise. Vampires weren't the forgiving sort.

"Thing is, I've been chatting with the ghost of the shooter, and it turns out we weren't some crime of circumstance. That demon thing that possessed me earlier sent him to kill Zane!"

"As part of a plot to get to you," Zane interjected, his voice gravelly in the recording. "Which is why you need to give me that phone."

Ella's voice got softer as if she held the phone away from her ear. "I can't give it to you. I'm talking to Felicia."

"No, you're talking to her voicemail. Hand it over. If we're being tracked, then we need to rid ourselves of the technology that might be at fault."

"Demons can't hack GPS locations."

"Do you know that for sure? Because I don't," he stated. "Hand it over."

"But I love my phone."

Felicia could imagine Ella hugging that stupid smartphone with its bedazzled pink cover. A present from Felicia who thought every woman should have pink jewels in their life.

"I'll get you a new one."

"But if I give it to you, how will Felicia call us back?"

"She won't. We'll contact her. Now hand it over."

"Make me," Ella said stubbornly, and probably still looking cute. "Zane! No. Eek!"

End of message.

Felicia frowned and replayed it. She didn't learn anything new. Next, she tried calling both Ella's and Zane's phones. They went straight to voicemail. Another call placed to Zane's home put her in touch with the very capable housekeeper.

Anna answered with a brisk, "You've reached the Langley residence. How may I help you?"

"I need to talk to Zane or Ella."

"I'm afraid the lord and lady are indisposed."

"Are they at home?" Felicia asked, irritation growing.

"No."

"You know who this is. So don't mess with me. I need to contact them. It's urgent."

"Does Madame wish to leave a message?"

"No, what I want is for you to tell me where Zane and Ella are. They're in need of my aid."

"If they want you to know their location, then they'll contact you."

Click.

As loyalty went, Zane's housekeeper was one of the best. A pity Felicia would have to kill her for being so insubordinate.

At least Felicia had some kind of assurance Zane and Ella were safe. Odd how she worried about their welfare. One might say she considered them friends. A queen usually eschewed those kinds of relationships, mostly because the majority of people she encountered only played nice that they might in turn use her. There was a certain cachet that came from being seen as in favor. But Zane...he'd never been interested in anything Felicia could give him. The only thing he ever asked for was help with Ella.

As for Ella...Felicia hated to admit it, but she liked her even as she sometimes wanted to throttle her. It fascinated her that Ella didn't fawn over Felicia. Didn't treat her like a queen at all. Anyone else would have lost their life for the temerity. But Ella was special, and powerful. If someone was targeting Zane in order to clear their way to grabbing Ella, then nefarious deeds were afoot.

And no one invited me.

Being the paranoid sort—which explained her longevity—she immediately wondered if whoever planned the ambush had designs on her throne. After all, she held one of the most esteemed positions in the supernatural underworld. Vampire Queen for North America, second in power only to the European King— who was older by a century and the winner of their wager; Marie Antoinette was indeed not wearing underpants at her execution.

Felicia's wrong guess meant she abandoned Europe —on a wooden boat with the hold packed tight with her belongings and servants—to live in the wilds.

Best thing ever.

In a funny twist of fate, her ignoble demotion was the thing that ended up making her more powerful on the world stage. Not only did the United States of America become a force to be reckoned with, her court wasn't mired in as many politics.

But that was only because she ruled with an iron fist.

Given Zane was one of her strongest, most loyal allies, harming him was, in fact, a blow against her throne. Was another vampire attempting a coup?

Except a vampire would have known a headshot required precision. Someone of Zane's age had excellent restoration abilities. Short of removing his head, burning it and his body, then scattering the ashes, you'd be hard-pressed to kill him.

So probably not a vampire. But someone willing to risk a queen's ire to get a hold of Ella. A cheerful woman with too much power at her fingertips. A sorceress who could cause a lot of damage if in the wrong hands.

Judging by the message, the attack was connected to Ella's earlier possession. Why? Where did this new enemy sprout from?

She wondered if Zane kept the shooter's body for evidence. She wouldn't mind a sniff and bite to find her own set of clues. Ella might talk to spirits, but Felicia's discerning palette could tell a lot, too. Associations with the wrong sort always left a flavor in the meat. Think of it as a marinade that was a little more complex than vinegars and spices.

Alas, Zane wasn't available, the human snack she had brought to her room didn't really satisfy, and sleep still eluded her. She paced, restless, wanting to do something.

Anything.

But she was stuck. It didn't take a vampire's special cognition to know that beyond her shaded windows the sun shone brightly. Driving around trying to avoid its laser-like rays wouldn't accomplish much other than to irritate her.

Sitting around waiting for any kind of news irritated as well. She needed distraction.

For some reason, dancing green eyes and a pointed beard came to mind.

Tariq never did fully explain why he'd appeared early. For all his teasing, she knew what time the delegation was set to arrive. They'd been travelling for days now. First by boat, then by train. Which made no sense given he'd popped in and out of her place with no problem.

Yet, they'd chosen one of the most sluggish methods to travel. She had one of her servants watching over the djinn as they made their way from the port in San Francisco cross country to her modest castle.

If by modest you considered sixteen bedrooms, twenty-one full bathrooms, a ballroom, three dining rooms, a conservatory, and her own theatre big enough to seat one hundred modest. Compared to the vampire king of the European states, she was living in a mere cottage. How she envied Raymond his authentic stone castle in the Swiss Alps.

Thinking of accommodations reminded her... She dialed the wizard who'd set the spell on her house.

The moment he answered, she said very calmly, "Puffbans Emporium of Magic, your spell failed."

"Impossible," he sputtered.

"A djinn not only made it past your wards but into my bedchamber."

"A genie? I thought they were extinct."

Since she could still smell the spice of him, she begged to disagree. "Not extinct, merely not interested in humankind. And he made it past the wards with ease."

"An anomaly."

"Was the evil spirit who possessed a guest of mine also an anomaly?"

"Are you actually claiming demonic possession?" The wizard snorted. "Please. Demons don't exist. They're a hoax meant to scare the religious into following the doctrines of churches."

Actually, demons did exist. They were just kind of useless. Mostly they worked security and were considered expendable. Funny how the legends had them painted as big and bad. "I never said it was a demon."

"Probably just a mere ghost then. I warned you the spells wouldn't stop them, and you were fine with that."

"Ghosts, yes. This was something else."

"Says you. Perhaps you are mistaken?"

She paused a moment. "Mistaken?" The word curled dangerously. "You will return the fee with interest unless you wish to have your blood used to power the new wards I'll have made."

"I will return your wretched money. Djinn and demons indeed."

Hanging up, Felicia tapped her chin. The human had given her food for thought. Demonic possession. Could it be? The ancient texts spoke of it happening. The demons of today might find themselves diluted, but what if a strong one existed? A demon more like the stories of old. A killing machine with the power to jump into a body.

Worrisome. Ella had a lot of potential power that wouldn't be good if controlled by the wrong parties.

Tapping her nails on her desk, Felicia fired off some messages. The first to her keeper of the archives. *Send me everything we have on demons.*

The second note went to her aesthetician. *I need a wax.* Because she couldn't rid her mind of those sexy green eyes and that smile. But what she could get rid of was the hair on her legs and mound.

When it came to arming herself, Felicia knew not all battles should be fought with fang and sword. Sometimes, the weapon between her legs was the mightiest of all.

FOUR

THE PLEASURE almost wasn't worth the fatigue. The journey to visit their hostess had taxed his magical reserves, and yet Tariq didn't feel he had a choice. How else to ensure their final destination would provide a safe haven?

Then again, there was no other valid option for sanctuary. The humans wouldn't provide succour to one of his ilk. More likely they'd try and dissect him, or have him accomplish impossible wishes, the kind that killed a djinn who expended all his magic.

Greedy humans.

Now more than ever he wanted to return to his bottle. Enjoy a few centuries of solitude with nothing but the classics playing and his books. Alas, he couldn't relax. Not until a certain crisis was averted.

His departure and return to the train went unnoticed by his companions, which disturbed him. Had they learned nothing yet of being vigilant? Apparently not, for his mates drowsed. He could understand the temptation. The lulling motion of the train could put anyone to sleep. Especially since the boredom was very real.

Two days now they'd been riding the rails across America. Big place, the USA. He'd not expected such size. Was it any wonder Tariq got impatient and popped ahead for a peek?

Probably better his travel mates remained unaware of his jaunt. They would chide him if they saw how he wasted his magic. And yes, they'd call it waste. They guarded theirs close. Hoarding every last bit.

As if that would do them any good. Now was the time for them to be bold. To act. Too long had they spent simply existing, apart from the world.

Who could blame them? For so long, the djinn had been slaves to the humans. All because their damned cousin became friends with that little thief, Aladdin. To think he'd had movies made about him. Made it seem like djinn granting wishes for humans was a good thing.

It wasn't. Ironic how the stories omitted the part where Aladdin's djinn had his magic stripped and was exiled to the Arctic. He didn't fare so well with the wildlife. When Tariq was young, his uncle told him that when the polar bears passed wind, the remnants of djinn magic colored the skies over the north. Ignorant scientists called it the aurora borealis.

Djinn called it polar farts. Which was funny, and yet the tale of the thief and the djinn was a warning to them all. Don't get caught and used by humans. The entire incident was also the reason they'd created new djinn laws that basically outlawed the giving of wishes. If the leprechauns could keep their gold and turn aside those following the rainbow, then the djinn could stop playing slave to humanity's whims.

Now his kind used magic for themselves.

See where this was going?

With no one to serve and no one to hold them accountable, the djinn grew lazy and complacent. The life of leisure and peace had that effect. Their birth rates, already low, dropped further. Their numbers dwindled. Their magic weakened from lack of true use. The last battle djinn—once a coveted role that required centuries of training—had died and with him the rantings of a time before this one. A time when they had to fight to survive.

A time that had returned to find no one prepared for it. Tariq closed off those memories rather than allow himself to dwell on the slaughter and his failure.

Azzam, chin tucked to his chest, snorted and snuffled before startling himself awake. He regarded Tariq through one eye, the one with the silver-sheened cataract. Azzam claimed it let him see things in the future. Let him see choices to be made for the greater good, that good being Azzam's, of course.

"Are we there yet?" grouched Azzam, shoving an elbow into Jamaal's midsection, startling him awake.

"No." Tariq leaned against the far wall, the beds tucked away to give them a semblance of space.

"We should have made the woman come to us."

Somehow, Tariq doubted that would have gone over well with the queen.

Jamaal yawned, the movement stretching the skin still scarring the left side of his face. No amount of healing could fix it. Who knew a fire existed that burned hot enough to harm a djinn? "Don't complain, Azzam. We'd be there already if you'd agreed to fly."

"Never!" Azzam grumbled. "Aeroplanes are unnatural. Only those with true wings should be able to fly."

"Then how do you explain the rug?" Tariq teased, the argument not a new one.

Azzam tilted his nose. "The rug does not fly. It merely defies the laws of gravity."

"Hypocrite," Tariq coughed into his fist and then bit back a smile at Azzam's glare. "A plane would have had us at our destination three days ago."

"And we'd probably be dead," Azzam spat. "Aeroplanes crash. They can also explode. We all know it doesn't take much."

"We could have driven," Jamaal interjected, "and cut the trip in half."

"Cars require a driver and are uncomfortable for long journeys."

Cars also didn't have a bathroom Azzam could use every second hour. The more he lost touch with his djinn essence, the more human and *old* he became. The hair that only a few weeks ago had been thick and dark now crowned Tariq's grandfather in silver. Creases lined his eyes and cheeks. Azzam no longer looked like an uncle to Tariq. He resembled a true grandfather. At last. And Tariq enjoyed taunting him with the title when it would have the most effect.

"You should have let me transport you."

"Djinn can't transport djinn." An odd fact few knew. They could grab hold of anything and anyone else and bring it with them when they traveled the spaces between. But djinn? It was like they were cemented in place. They didn't move anywhere.

But grandfather was almost human. Would that quirk still apply? Tariq could see the magic core of him ripped and bleeding magic. In the battle that sent them fleeing their home, Azzam had lost a huge piece of it. The chunk of ragged core that remained couldn't seem to heal or replenish itself.

His grandfather was magically bleeding to death. Or, in this case, losing what made him djinn, which, in turn, led him into humanity.

Tariq's brother, Jamaal, wasn't much better off. He had a bigger chunk left of his magic, but he bled as well and created a trail. One that Tariq worked hard to contain and disperse lest their enemies appear to finish them off.

"We've almost arrived. We'll be there by the end of the day."

"Taking succour with a vampire." Grandfather snorted. It didn't have the rakish elegance he used to employ with the ladies. It was more of a harrumph that shook his long white beard.

"Where else would you like us to go?" There were

no other djinn enclaves left that he knew of. The one in Italy found itself attacked as well. The two surviving djinn from that tragedy had fled to the European king, and disappeared en route. As far as he was concerned, the only ones left of his kind were Tariq, Grandfather, and Jamaal, and they were still in danger with no safe haven. Given their solitude, they no longer had any allies to call upon for help.

"Damned elves. Still blaming us for the split." There was a reason people used the expression "Be careful what you wish for." In this case, the elves had made a wish to keep their Summerlands safe and hidden from everyone. However, they didn't add the proper clauses.

The Summerland portals disappeared from Earth, locking the elves out. No amount of yelling or wishing again could change that. Oddly enough, the spell didn't stop people from leaving the Summerlands.

They just couldn't return.

Of course, they blamed the djinn.

"The vampire queen was the only one that did not ignore our request." All his other notes were refused. She was his last hope.

"Negotiating with someone who might discover our blood is the ambrosia they've never even dreamed of seems non-conducive to a prolonged future." This from Jamaal. "Then again, I hear their feeding can feel better than any orgasm. Perhaps it won't be so bad. I hear the vampire queen is attractive."

She was. Very. But not just because of her body.

Bodies were so easily sculpted. The mind, though, the will and the power behind actual intelligence, that wasn't something you could create. It either existed or it didn't. And finding a unique flavor of personality, one not awed by his djinn genes, or immediately asking for favors, intrigued.

"We are not seducing our only possible ally," Tariq commanded.

"Why not?" Jamaal asked. "Sex can be a powerful way to bind."

"Leave the queen alone." Tariq might have barked the command a little more forcefully than necessary.

Jamaal eyed him, but it was Grandfather who spoke. "The boy is hiding something." Azzam focused on him, squinting his silvery eye.

"Hiding what?" Jamaal inhaled, and his lips pulled into a smile, the scarred corner extending it into a parody of what it once was. "Is it me, or do I smell perfume in the cab? Dear brother, did you entertain someone while we slept? Which would be interesting given we bought all the available berths on this train so they'd remain empty."

Expensive, but it made monitoring for attacks much easier. They'd thought about hiring mercenaries upon starting the voyage cross country, however a problem with sailors coming over—namely those sailors trying to sink the ship—showed the danger in doing that.

The issue with lying was he'd be caught. So he didn't bother. "I might have gone ahead to scout."

"You left!" Jamaal accused.

"Only for a short while."

"You shouldn't have left at all," Jamaal rebuked. "You are supposed to be conserving your magic." Was that the real reason, or was Jamaal more concerned about the fact he hadn't noticed Tariq's departure? That he was losing his ability to sense? Did his brother fear being alone if something happened?

"We're close. It didn't take much effort to pop in and out."

"Was it worth it?"

Recalling the kiss, he said, "Yes," without thinking, and must have shown a hint of his thoughts.

"Sniffing at her skirts already. Thatta boy." Grandfather slapped his thigh. "No sex, indeed. I knew you had to be joking. Plow her good and she'll do anything you ask."

"I'm not plowing anyone."

"Then I'll do it. Women are always wanting to rub me for luck." Azzam winked.

Quickly, Tariq barked, "Don't you dare ask her to rub you!"

"Then I'll offer to pleasure her. This tongue knows its way around a woman." His grandfather pursed his lips, and Tariq might have vomited if he'd had something in his stomach.

Instead, he scrubbed a hand through his hair. "Watch your language. You know you can't say that. Especially not in America. You'll get lynched."

"Since when is wanting to show appreciation for the female form a crime?"

"Since they asked us to stop."

Jamaal smirked. "Does this mean they'll stop pinching your ass and inviting you for drinks in their rooms later on?"

"They'd better not stop." It made figuring out who was willing easier if the woman made the first move.

"Since you've met her, how is our hostess?" Jamaal leaned back, hands folded over his stomach.

Cute and feisty. "Somewhat well guarded. House defenses were adequate against most threats." Except the one they faced.

"And the woman herself?"

Off-limits. A thought that startled. He ignored it to instead reply, "Quick-thinking. I can see why she's lasted this long."

"Think she can help?"

Tariq shrugged. "Maybe. She at least has access to an army, and connections to the other groups that have shunned us."

"Bastards. See if we give them any wishes," Azzam grumbled. "I'll set them on fire myself and refuse to piss on them."

"No setting anyone on fire. We can't afford any more enemies. If we lack allies, it is our own fault for being segregated for so long."

"I miss my bottle," complained Azzam.

They all did.

The train, what had been chugging along at a

steady speed, suddenly lurched before slowing to a stop.

What was happening? They still had hours to go to their destination.

Tariq immediately cast out his senses. Unlike his family, his magic was still intact and functioning. If a little depleted from his teleportation stunt.

He could have cursed in seven languages and thirteen dialects when he saw the converging vehicles, their combustion engines bright orange flares in the esoteric field all around them. The humans were more of a blue-green smudge. At least two dozen of them, probably armed.

"We've got company," he grimly announced.

"And I've got a Glock." Jamaal pulled it from the bag he kept at his feet. He flipped off the safety and held it up with a smile.

"Since when do you carry a gun?" Tariq asked.

"Since I can't conjure a sword out of my ass."

Not having magic put his brother at a disadvantage in a fight. "You can't shoot them all before they manage to harm us." Which Tariq could survive, but Grandfather and Jamaal with their broken magic? That kind of injury could be the thing that set them on the final path.

Then Tariq would be alone. Alone to fight. The only djinn left to repopulate the world and avoid extinction. Him, a father?

He'd best make sure his family survived to carry on tradition.

"Maybe they're here to escort us." He put that ridiculous notion forward, knowing it would help focus his grandfather.

"Idiot. Escorts don't stop trains in the middle of nowhere. We are under attack. Send forth the centaurs." Azzam waved his arm. Nothing happened.

"We don't have centaurs." They'd actually gone extinct a few centuries ago. Human males hunted them down and slaughtered them all. The expression "hung like a horse"... Given their inadequacy, the humans felt a need to restore their masculinity by eliminating the competition.

"Send out the dancers then. Let them hypnotize the enemy into putting down their weapons."

First off, that only ever worked once, on a tribe of lonely Titans. "We have no dancers. It's just us, Azzam. And only I have magic."

"Which does us no good since you can't kill humans with it."

Another djinn quirk. They couldn't directly use their powers to kill. If the effect of something resulted in death, then so be it, but he couldn't just toss lightning bolts at humans and knock them off their vehicles.

He could, however, nudge a boulder off a cliff. He only needed to find a cliff.

"What else would you like me to do?" Asked a moment before a hail of gunfire strafed the train car. They all hit the floor and huddled inside a shield cocoon Tariq spun for them.

"I've got enough juice to pop out if you take him." Jamaal angled his head to Azzam.

"You can't take me. I'm a djinn." The claim emerged quavering and afraid. Over the centuries, Tariq had never seen the mighty Azzam afraid of anything. Then *the enemy* arrived and soundly defeated them. Now, the more Grandfather lost touch with his magic, the more human he appeared.

Human enough to transport? Jamaal thought it might be possible, even as the idea obviously terrified his grandfather.

Even if Tariq wasn't able to transport Azzam, Jamaal needed to escape before he overtaxed what was left of his magic.

More bullets peppered the train. Tariq's shield absorbed the impact, but for how long? He couldn't hold out forever.

"Can you make it to the vampire enclave on your own?" he asked Jamaal.

"I can, but"—Jamaal arched a brow—"you're sure this queen can help us?"

"She's the only one who can," asserted Azzam, the most vocal opponent of their meeting, and yet the one who also kept claiming the queen was needed if they were to survive.

"Go," Tariq urged. "I'll be right behind you."

Jamaal gave him a hard stare. "Don't be a hero."

"I would never even think of it."

"Don't make me yank your spirit from the netherworld for a beating," Jamaal threatened. "I'll expect to see you momentarily."

Closing his eyes, Jamaal appeared to clench and relax all at once. Tariq could see the strain and the ballooning of magic out of him as he pulled enough together to send himself elsewhere.

Pop. The displacement wasn't neat. He'd not seen his brother this sloppy since their days in the schoolroom. A long, long time ago. They'd learned finesse since then.

"Our turn, old man."

"It won't work," Azzam claimed when Tariq turned his gaze on him.

"We're still going to try. Hold on to me."

"I am not a weak woman who needs you to rescue me."

"Another thing you can't say," Tariq announced with a sigh.

"So many rules. They should have never let them leave the kitchen. Education and equal rights indeed," Azzam grumbled.

"We don't have time for this. We need to try."

"If you insist. But I am not clinging to you. It's undignified. You can hold me."

Tariq wanted to wrap his hands around his grandfather's stubborn neck. How long since he and Azzam had been in such close proximity? Three centuries, four. It might have been more if they hadn't been attacked.

He grabbed his grandfather by the arms, closed his

own damned eyes, and yanked on as much magic as he could find. Perhaps if he powered it enough.

Nothing happened.

Azzam snickered. "Still a djinn." Said in an "I told you so" tone.

"Would have been better if you weren't," Tariq snapped. Now he'd have to find a way to get them out of here and to safety. Without directly killing any of the humans with magic.

"Conjure me a sword, and we'll fight like our ancestors."

"You can't use a blade against a bullet." Nor did their blades work on humans. A gun would work since the bullet, once fired, was independent and not magic based; however, Tariq had never practiced, and his last attempt resulted in a hole in their ship. "What we need is a carpet."

Since they didn't have one, he settled for a seat. Tariq rose to his feet, reshaping his shielding cocoon with him, trying to ignore the way it shuddered with the impact of the bullets. The humans fired round after round. The walls of the train were riddled with holes. Daylight streamed in.

He gripped one of the seats and pulled hard. It didn't budge. "Unbolt yourself at once." He shoved the wish at the chair and a moment later, held it aloft. "Sit in it."

Azzam shook his head. "I am not flying in that."

"Oh yes you are." Because spells didn't work on djinn either. He couldn't make Azzam fly, or even himself. Dissipate into a mist, yes, but that wasn't practical for travel. Strong winds had been known to cause injury to djinn who weren't careful. Carpets were considered a classic way to move around. But anything could technically be used: brooms, sleds, even beanbag chairs.

He just needed an object to enchant. The chair hovered, and his grandfather clung to its armrests, glowering. "This is undignified."

"A simple 'thank you' would suffice. Once you're clear of the bullets, the chair should make its way straight to the queen's home. Try not to fall off."

"How about you? I don't see you sitting in a chair."

"I'll be along shortly. First I need to cover your retreat." Before grandfather could complain, Tariq sealed him in a shield. A soundproof one that also deflected sight. But it wouldn't protect Azzam from stray shots. The limitations of magic.

Which was why Tariq would provide a distraction. He waved a hand forward and peeled back the metal of the car, catching the attention of the ambush gathered. He waved at the gaping mercenaries drawing their fire —who surely, despite their possessed minds, must wonder at what happened. Magic was a thing for movies and books, not real life.

With them occupied, he tore a hole in the roof of the train and sent Azzam rocketing into the sky.

That left just him and the small army.

He smiled amidst the gunfire strafing his shield and

boomed in a voice that carried, "Who's going to tell me who hired you?"

When they replied with even more bullets, he responded with a reflective shield, bouncing the missiles back to their senders. Body armor caught the majority, but more than a few fell as well. Screams and groans took the place of the noise of combustion weapons firing.

He boomed again. "Who hired you?"

It wasn't until only one attacker was left, lying on the ground, lips bubbling with blood, that he got an answer. Tariq knelt on the field of carnage. Not his fault the humans hadn't learned their lesson after the first two rounds of gunfire. And who knew a rolling train engine would take down more humans than bowling pins?

"Who do you work for?"

With eyes sparking red in the center, the soldier's bloody lips parted and whispered, "Your doom."

FIVE

THERE WAS NO POUNDING this time to warn her. Simply a shriek from her major-domo. He didn't like being startled, which made her wonder how anyone managed. Usually Ainsley answered the door before people could even lift a fist to knock.

Could it be...?

She almost slapped her hand as it rose to pat at her hair. She remained seated on her sofa as Ainsley appeared at the door, his expression grave, the epitome of a good manservant. His lessons from Zane's prim and proper Hendricks were paying off.

"My queen, you have a visitor. Where do you wish to—?"

"No time for that." A man shoved past him, and she was struck by two things: One, he was quite lovely with a light brown complexion and dashing earring in his ear, and two, he was a djinn. Not the same one as before, though.

"Who are you?" And where was Tariq?

"I am Jamaal, and you must be the delightful queen I heard nothing about." He grabbed her hand, and she allowed him to kiss the back of it, the soft press of his lips a contrast to the twisted skin of the scar across half his face.

"You're early." Late afternoon wasn't seven p.m.

"I would have been earlier, but I had to make a few stops along the way. Where are Azzam and Tariq?"

"How would I know?"

He gave her a sharp glance. "I was supposed to meet them here."

"Weren't you travelling together?"

"We were until the ambush occurred and we were separated."

She blinked. "What ambush?"

"The one on the train. Which isn't important. What is salient is the fact Tariq should have been here by now."

"He was this morning. But he left."

"Not that visit." The djinn named Jamaal paced. "That bastard stayed behind, I'll wager. Took them on all by himself. Thinks I can't handle a few bullets." Said in a disgruntled grumble.

"Someone was shooting at you?" She tried to piece together the story.

"Our train car looked like Swiss cheese when I left."

"I didn't think you could be killed that easily."

Even vampires could handle gunfire. It was beheading and daylight that were the real issues.

"Under normal circumstances, we aren't."

Good to know this wasn't normal. Then again, she'd kind of guessed that given the djinn were the ones to contact her out of the blue. "Are you under attack? Is someone targeting you?"

"Did the scars give it away?" He pointed mockingly to his face.

She barely gave the marks a second glance. People with long lives didn't remain unscathed. She had the mark of the cross burned in one thigh by a zealous priest. "Who is hunting you? Humans?" Because his description of the ambush thus far seemed to point at them.

"If only it were just humans. We could handle them. Alas, we are being decimated by the only thing strong enough to counter our magic," said Jamaal.

"Who?" She tapped her foot impatiently as he resorted to drawing out the drama. "Get to the point."

But it wasn't Jamaal who answered.

"Not who, what. Demons," announced Tariq as he strode into the room.

"Does no one know how to knock and wait to be announced?" she declared, only to be ignored.

Tariq chose to address Jamaal. "You made it unharmed, I see. Excellent. Where is Grandfather?"

"How would I know? I left him with you. Don't tell me you lost him."

"Maybe. I was busy keeping those hell-spawned

demons from jumping into new bodies and following Azzam."

"They're still after us?"

"Who's after you?" Felicia asked. "Would someone bloody well tell me what's happening?"

Tariq turned his gaze on her, the playful shine of the morning replaced with a serious mien. "It's a long story."

"Try giving me a condensed version."

"Demons. Possession. Eradication of my kind. Now if you don't mind, I'll explain more later. Right now, I need to locate Azzam."

Given he'd stolen whatever retort she had with his claim, she kept her lips shut as Tariq closed his eyes. Whatever he did—magic, or something else—caused his scent to spike.

Delicious. She almost licked her lips.

He snapped his eyes open suddenly and declared, "He's almost here. I'd better go meet him."

"I'll tell the gate to let his car past." She slid her finger across the screen of her phone to notify the gatehouse.

"He's not arriving by conventional means. How do we access your rooftop terrace?"

She didn't ask how he knew about it. Her garden atop the house wasn't exactly a secret. "Why?"

"You'll see."

See what? Curiosity made her say, "You can reach it only through my bedroom. If you'll both follow me."

"Two of us. Kinky," Jamaal teased.

Felicia shot him a glare as she passed him. "If you're not male enough to satisfy me on your own, then you don't belong in my bed." She never was one to share. But her gaze softened as it swept past Jamaal to Tariq. "Do you remember the way?"

"As if I'd forget. After you." He swept a bow and waggled a brow at her as she strode past. She wondered if she imagined the heat of his stare on her backside. She also wondered if he'd cast some djinn lust spell on her to make her panties wet. If he thought bedding her would be that easy, then she'd have to show him. Just because she had her legs stripped of hair didn't mean he wouldn't have to work to see them wrapped around his waist.

Arriving at the bedroom, she flung open the double doors and entered a sanctuary that was...

"Holy Muhammad and his concubines. It's like a bottle of Pepto barfed all over her room," Jamaal exclaimed.

Not quite. There were many white and silver accents to break up the preponderance of pink. She liked it. It was her girly sanctuary away from the politics of court.

"I'm going to guess you like the color pink," Tariq stated.

"Don't act so surprised. You saw it this morning."

"Briefly, and at the time I was more focussed on the fact you thought you could choke me to death one-handed."

She tilted her chin. "I have been told I am strong."

The exact term usually also included freakish when she had to display said strength.

"You're also cute when you're just woken up."

Such an utterly stupid and masculine thing for him to say and yet it shut her mouth more effectively than any insult.

"The roof terrace is through there." The massive sliding doors could retract into the walls and open up her room to the garden she'd created outside. In the daytime, metal shades locked over them.

Some legends persisted in putting vampires underground to avoid daylight. Those people obviously never survived a cave-in. Much easier to escape from the top floor of a house than when you were buried under tons of its rubble.

She took her time following Tariq and his long-legged stride. Jamaal caught up to him. With the brothers standing side by side, she noted some of their similarities. The build of their bodies, with Jamaal a touch slimmer. They both had dark hair, with Tariq choosing to keep his trimmer. He also sported a beard and moustache, whereas Jamaal kept his jaw clean-shaven.

No denying they were related, and now they awaited the arrival of their grandfather, another djinn. Would he arrive via something rustic like a Turkish carpet? Or would he be more extravagant and coast in on the back of a dragon? Or was she being speciesist? Could be he hired a helicopter and would jump out.

One thing was for sure, the djinn were nothing as

expected, and more interesting than she could have hoped.

She leaned against a column of Grecian stone, an authentic antique. Costly, too, given she bought it from an excavation that went to auction on the black market. It formed part of the pergola that provided shade for her delicate skin.

The djinn didn't fear the sunlight. They stood tall in it, faces turned to the sky, arguing in low tones.

"I can't believe you did that to Azzam. He is going to kill you," Jamaal snickered.

"He's alive. He can be grateful."

"Azzam grateful?" For some reason, both the men laughed at the thought.

But that laughter died as Tariq announced, "He's here."

One moment the sky was still clear, those nasty rays waiting to singe her skin if she stepped out into the light, and then the next, there was a chair in the sky.

A literal seat torn from something, the base of it was a pair of metal tracks. Sitting within its padded comfort, an old man, his robes a dark navy trimmed in silver, his beard pointed and long, the top of his head covered in a ball cap.

The floating seat landed in her garden, and then she was treated to the old fellow leaping from it and cuffing Tariq on the arm.

"Don't you ever do that again!"

"You're welcome."

"Welcome for what? It rained." The man they called Azzam pointed to his robes.

"You dried." Tariq's dry reply.

"No thanks to you. You should have let me stay behind and help you fight those men."

"Fight?" Tariq queried. "I did no such thing."

"Did they die?" Azzam snapped.

"I merely defended myself. It was their own fault they died. All they had to do was stop firing their guns."

"How many did you kill?" Felicia waved a hand. "Forget that. Doesn't matter. Who did they work for, and more importantly, will they follow your trail here?" Felicia fired the questions at him because it became clear whatever shit had sent him fleeing from his country had followed.

"Are you afraid, my mighty vampire queen?"

Her turn to show disdain. "Merely wondering if we should pack the antiques so they don't get damaged in any coming battles." She was still peeved at the loss of the Ming vase during World War II.

"You should be afraid because even you and all your minions can't stop the coming menace."

"Would you like some ominous music with your announcement?" She arched a brow. "That was seriously cliché."

"But true. A great danger is coming, a threat to everyone, not just djinn."

"I know, you already said it. Demons. And too late, my bottle-loving, bearded guest, I've already met one."

SIX

"MET ONE?" Tariq blinked at Felicia and couldn't help but enjoy the sight of her again. Just the right height to tuck under his chin, with long dark hair and a shapely figure. While her appearance might be that of a young woman, forever frozen in time, her eyes and expression held the wisdom and intelligence of age. "When did you see the demon? Have they already begun to strike?" He'd thought the problem still contained to the Middle East. Then again, the attack today showed the enemy's powers were beginning to creep farther and farther.

"I met it a few hours before your first visit."

"How did you survive?" Then his brow darkened, and he held out his hand and called forth a sword, one that flamed on the sharp edge. "Are you allied with the foul creatures?"

Her eyes widened, and then her full lips parted to release a throaty laugh. "Allied with demons? Did the lack of oxygen in your bottle addle your wits? Of course I'm not working with them. I said I met one. Damned thing possessed a friend of mine to give us a message."

"What did it say?"

"Not much. Basically, 'We're coming for you.'"

Tariq frowned. A fiend giving warning? "You claim it spoke through your friend. Is she allied with demons?"

"Ella?" The queen snorted. "Hardly. It possessed her, and she tossed it. Then it possessed someone else and tried to kill Zane. Which wasn't a brilliant thing to do. It's dead now."

"Doubtful it died. Their spirit usually moves on to another host. Who are this Ella and Zane?" Tariq asked.

"People I need to talk to."

"I agree. Have them fetched at once." Tariq forgot himself for a moment and commanded the queen.

She arched a brow. "Excuse me, but you don't give the orders around here."

"Very well. You can demand their presence. But we must make haste. I don't know if we have much time. Our journey took longer than expected." The last jab was aimed at his grandfather, who pretended innocence.

"I can't order them to come because I don't know where they are. After the attack, they went into hiding. I was planning to go find them once the sun goes down. You can come with me if you'd like."

"Leave? But we've just arrived." And while he retained enough of his pride to not complain, he did feel fatigue pulling. Djinn were powerful, but even they required rest and sustenance, especially after expending great amounts of magic.

"Then I guess I'll go alone."

Forget getting any rest. "If you're going, then I'm coming with you."

"Me too," Jamaal declared.

As for Azzam, he grimaced. "I am not chasing a skirt looking for peons." Which, given the weariness enhancing his wrinkles, translated to: I'm old and need a nap.

"Jamaal, stay here with him." Tariq jerked his head at Azzam. "Make sure he doesn't cause another lawsuit by pinching the maids' cheeks again."

Jamaal opened his mouth to argue, and Tariq shook his head. "Rest. I'll be back."

As he turned to join Felicia, they were all startled by a bright voice exclaiming, "Where's everyone going? Can I come?"

He froze as he noticed the petite woman framed by the pink bedroom at her back. A woman he never noticed approaching. A woman who sent a chill through him.

There was nothing menacing about her. He could blow her over with a single breath. She appeared fragile and almost fey-like. Yet that was just a sham. She was power. He saw it, saw past her fleshy dimension to another level, where she glowed all the colors of a rainbow, only caught in tiny glimpses through the maelstrom of gray smoke swirling around her.

"What is she?" He'd never seen the like.

But his grandfather had. "A witch!" He pointed a finger.

"If you say 'burn the witch,' I will kill you." A man stepped to the woman's side, his eyes dark with the cold promise of death. He angled himself protectively in front of the petite blonde.

Azzam chuckled. "Burn her? Why would I kill our only salvation?"

Hard to reply to that kind of thing, but Jamaal managed. "What did you put in your cereal today? Because the crazy coming out of your mouth is off the charts even for you."

"I am not crazy."

Looking at the queen, Tariq mouthed, "Yes he is." To which he got a smile. One that even managed to reach her eyes. He found himself staring. Mesmerized.

Which confused him. Since when did that happen? Usually, he was the one captivating women. Yet, here he found himself drawn to five feet of curves and courage. He couldn't forget how she'd fearlessly gone after him with a firm grip. She never once wavered even though he wished upon her his most successful smoldering gaze.

She didn't melt and take off that ridiculous sleeping gown. What woman wore such a voluminous thing? She belonged in lingerie, or nothing at all.

Yet, at the same time, he'd never seen anything so

arousing. In his recollection, he could almost make out her willowy shape through the gauzy fabric.

And now she wore something just as ridiculous. Linen slacks with wide legs, cinched at her waist, her flowered blouse tucked in, the buttons done almost to the neck. Did she do it on purpose to seduce with her attire?

"Ella. Zane," the queen exclaimed. "I was about to go looking for you."

"You would have had a hard time finding us. We spent the day in seclusion," Zane proffered.

"In a hotel. With a Jacuzzi tub and room service." The small woman named Ella blushed. "We didn't leave all day."

The queen ignored that to get to the point. "I got the message about Zane being shot. Are you fully healed?" Felicia approached the couple and gripped Zane by the jaw. She turned his face and eyed a spot on his cheek that appeared discolored compared to the rest of him.

"I am—" Zane began, only to have Ella interrupt.

"Someone shot him. In the face!"

"They obviously didn't have good aim." Jamaal felt compelled to interject.

"Actually, they did. I almost died, but Ella saved me."

That caught Felicia's attention for some reason. She turned to the woman. "What did you do?"

"I don't know." The petite woman shrugged.

"You healed him."

"Maybe. Just a little. He mostly healed himself."

"Only because she managed to somehow remove the worst of the brain damage," Zane interjected "What should have taken days or weeks to recover from took only minutes."

Ella clung to Zane's arm. "He was so hungry after, too. Good thing the ghosties grabbed hold of the shooter. Zane needed him for a snack," Ella announced, as if eating a person was the most natural thing in the world. Then again, given her mate was a vampire, it probably was.

Felicia continued to question Ella. "I never knew you could use your powers to heal."

"Me either." She shrugged. "And before you ask, I have no idea how I did it. I just got upset, and it happened."

"Happened?" Tariq queried. "Magic doesn't just happen. It needs form and structure."

"Maybe for other people. Me, I kind of wing it." A bright smile went with the declaration.

"Healing wasn't the only thing she did." Zane angled his head at his wife. "Tell them what happened to the car."

"I'd rather not. She'll get mad," Ella said in a loud whisper with a glance at Felicia.

The queen crossed her arms. "What else did you do?"

"Well, once Zane went all fanged and jumped out of the car to eat his shooter, I might have had a bit of a panic attack and peeled open the car like a sardine can."

A sigh escaped Felicia. "What did I say about using your powers in noticeable ways?"

"Zane helped me take care of it. We sank it in a nearby swamp."

"The car is still registered to him."

"Maybe no one will find it."

The queen flung up her hands. "I give up. Doesn't anyone read anything about modern forensics?"

"We were working under pressure," Ella grumbled. "Now, if you're done giving me heck, why are you outside during daylight? And who are these people in your bedroom?" Her eyes widened. "Did we interrupt something?"

As Felicia gasped, "No," Tariq couldn't help but sidle close, slide an arm around her waist, and purr, "Yes."

She elbowed him, and while it didn't hurt, it did make him chuckle.

Stiff at his side, Felicia replied, "No, you didn't interrupt. It's just the djinn contingent who arrived somewhat earlier and via unexpected methods."

"Real genies?" Ella's eyes lit, and Tariq almost groaned because sure enough—

"Did that child just call us...g...g..." Azzam couldn't say it.

"That child is a ridiculously powerful ánima veneficus, which means she can slap you on the butt and call you Sally if she likes," Felicia said dryly.

"But why would I do that?" Ella's nose crinkled, making her look even more innocuous. How powerful could someone that cute be? Still, this was who the queen had insisted they find. What luck she came to them. Now perhaps they could get down to business.

"We've located your allies. Now what?" Tariq asked. "Do you have a plan to help us fight the demons?"

"No. Up until a few hours ago, I thought they were ugly bodyguards used by the dwarves. Suddenly, it turns out they can take over bodies."

"They are possessing those with flesh only until they can free their own. There is a crack in the seal keeping them prisoners. If we cannot repair it, then they will spill into our world," Azzam announced. Tariq didn't bother asking how his grandfather knew. It wasn't worth the cuff.

"Can't you just pour some cement into the crack?" Ella asked, earning a few stares. "What?"

"It's a rift into another dimension," Jamaal retorted. "It's going to need more than some quick fix. Not to mention we have to find it first."

"It's in the desert," his grandfather offered, not being helpful at all.

"If the demon crack is in the desert, then why are they possessing Ella here in America?" Felicia asked, a frown creasing her brow.

"Because their plan is to spread all over the world."

"Why?" Ella asked.

Azzam sputtered. "What do you mean why? Because that is what demons do."

"Why can't they live amongst us? Nothing wrong with diversity." The very innocent nature of Ella's question didn't prevent it sounding ridiculous.

"Demons are killers. Because of them, we have no home. No people. And we are just the start," Tariq announced, his tone grim. "Which is why we're here. We need help fighting them."

"Fight?" Ella's head tilted back, and her voice emerged several octaves lower. "You'll never win. I am the adversary, and you will spill your blood to free me."

SEVEN

CHANNELLING A DEMON, quite possibly from another dimension, had a way of changing how people looked at you. Ella wasn't surprised at all to see everyone gaping at her.

"She is possessed!" The genie's giant sword swung, only to be blocked as her ghostly friends formed a shield before her. Good thing they also held Zane back because he snarled at the attempt.

"Would you both stop it? I am not possessed." At the moment. But Mr. Rude-Pants-Demon was starting to annoy with his attempts to jump into her body.

"But you don't deny the demons are using you as a conduit," stated the genie.

"Tariq, leave Ella alone. She's not the enemy," Felicia barked.

Not today she wasn't, but tell that to his wide-eyed, suspicious gaze. You'd think she'd be used to the way people looked at her by now.

How many times had she done something at the asylum? Something *weird* even by their standards, which got her put in solitary—a.k.a a room with padded walls chasing butterflies because of the drugs. Her friends in the attic loved to play pranks. Never mind they got Ella in trouble. Their petty games amused them in the afterlife, and Ella got used to people staring at her—and calling for her to die.

What she didn't expect was an old man, who looked like he'd stepped out of the Bible with his long beard and robes, to beam. "The gods are smiling upon us. A soul witch to save us all."

Not exactly the kind of endorsement she'd expected, but it would look cool on T-shirts.

"What are you saying, old man?" Tariq turned his green gaze onto the other guy.

"That she is the reason we came here. The one who can help us."

"Her?" asked the tall genie, his gaze intent. "What kind of forces do you wield? Have you fought demons before?" As he hammered Ella with questions, she could feel the heat rolling off of him in huge waves. The pungent aroma of cinnamon made her yearn for icing-covered hot cross buns. Mmm.

Poor Zane must have caught some of her interest because he bristled and stepped in front of her. "Slow down, Aladdin."

"Aladdin was the thief. Malik was the djinn in that travesty."

"Don't care. Back away from my wife."

Yes, wife. In a lovely midnight and moonlight ceremony attended by three hundred of their closest paranormal friends. The pool had to be drained the next day after the mess the mermaids made.

The old fellow held up his hands in a conciliatory gesture. "You misunderstand. We don't wish her harm. She might be the only one who can help us. So say the gods."

"Gods?" Zane scoffed. "Don't tell me the mighty djinn believe in those fables."

"Just because many have passed from this world doesn't mean they don't exist. There are still a few."

"And you know them?" Ella asked.

The old guy nodded. "Yes."

Felicia interjected herself. "Gods are all well and good, but they're not the issue right now. Ella, Zane, meet my guests. Tariq, Jamaal, and Azzam."

"I don't care about their names. What do you know of the demons?" Zane asked. "Why are they harassing my wife?"

The younger man with the scarred countenance, who must be Jamaal, turned his sloe-eyed gaze on Zane. "I don't know why they would want a human witch, but I would imagine it has much to do with her magic."

"The demons need all the magic they can muster," the old guy muttered.

"What for, Azzam?" Felicia asked.

"Freedom, of course. It is why they attacked the djinn first, for our magic is mightiest." Azzam puffed out his chest, which might have been more impressive had it not sported bird poop on it.

Tariq sighed. "We only have theories about the demons' motive. What we do know is they have captured all the bottles they could find and killed the djinn who opposed them. We three are the last free djinn that I know of. Given they hunt us still, I fear we might not be for long."

"Aha. I was right. You did drag trouble with you." Felicia jabbed a finger at his chest, not daunted at all by the fact the guy was way taller and a genie. Which Ella was pretty sure trumped vampire. But the queen didn't seem to care. She was utterly fearless.

Ella wanted to be Felicia when she grew up.

"Our trouble now," Tariq remarked. "But it will become your issue once we are out of the way. The demons we encountered are relentless."

"What do they want?" A question that kept coming back.

Jamaal sneered. "Everything. They've breached our world and plan to conquer it."

Ella clapped her hands. "Oh, wow, this is just like an episode of *Ash Versus the Evil Dead*."

Zane leaned close. "Not really. Demons don't turn people into zombies."

"Yet." She held up a hand. "But they can possess people and make them do stuff. They did it to the genie staff. That's how Tariq's people got taken."

His mouth rounded. "How did you know?"

"Esfir told me."

"Who?" Tariq asked.

Zane replied for her. "One of her ghosts."

That had all three of the genies staring at Ella. It probably didn't bode well that they were so impressed.

"For real?" Jamaal asked.

"I told you she was a soul sorceress." The vampire queen almost rolled her eyes.

Tariq faced her. "I thought you were perhaps mistaken in your application of the title. It's been a long time since one of her kind roamed the earth."

"They are rare," Azzam added to the conversation. "So rare that finding you might not be enough. The last time the demons managed to penetrate our world, a coven of thirteen converged upon the rift and used their combined power over the dead to seal it."

"Thirteen?" Tariq exclaimed. "You mean we need to find twelve more? How is it you're only mentioning this now?"

Azzam shrugged. "I thought the soul witches extinct. But where there is one…there could be others. We must simply find them."

"How?" snapped Tariq. "It's not as if we can place an advertisement seeking them."

"Wouldn't do you any good," Ella chimed in. "According to my friends, I'm the only one. But if it makes you feel better, they say I'm strong."

"One strong sorceress isn't the twelve needed for a spell. We are well and truly doomed." Tariq rubbed his face. "We wasted our time coming here."

"Why did you come here?" Zane asked. "Why travel so far?"

"Because my grandfather"—Tariq glared at the fellow—"had a vision that our only hope of survival was with the vampire queen."

"I'm pretty sure whatever survival he was talking about isn't going to be found in my bedroom," snapped Felicia. "Can we move this somewhere else? Say like a room meant for the telling of stories."

In other words, the library. Ella's favorite room in the house because it not only spanned three stories, with floor-to-super-high-ceiling bookcases, it also had ladders. On rails!

Ella only wished she had a decent singing voice for when she went wheeing around the room.

But today wasn't a day for a ladder race with Felicia. Who wasn't uptight when just the pair of them hung out.

Today they had to do serious talk.

At least nowadays when Ella had serious conversations, it wasn't with a doctor trying to increase the number of pills she took. Her asylum days were over. Zane had saved her. Helped her to find herself. And love.

"...and now we live super happily together in Zane's giant house. Which would be even more awesome if he let me get a kitten," she exclaimed as she regaled the genies with the story of her life.

They were awestruck and silent. The ghosts were

sobbing around her and attacking the spirits that ridiculed. Ella's childhood was nothing to mock.

"No cats. I'm allergic," Zane claimed.

"Which is totally unfair. You have werewolves."

"Who would eat a kitten," he argued, not for the first time.

"Not if I got a big one. With stripes." Ella offered him a smile and a bat of her lashes.

He groaned. "For the last time, I am not getting you a tiger or a lion, moonbeam."

"You will get me a pet."

"He will," agreed Azzam with a sage nod of his head. "Two of them. So say the gods."

Ella clapped her hands. "Yay."

"No."

"Can we get back to the demon problem?" said the serious spoilsport named Tariq. And here she'd thought him brave and playful when he dared to touch Felicia without permission. Ella had seen people lose arms and get beaten with them for less.

Ella cocked her head as a voice, reedy and thin with age, whispered in her special ear. "Esfir says it all began with an excavation and a tomb. Just like a movie." It made Ella long for an Indiana Jones whip and hat or the long cool hair of Angelina Jolie in *Tomb Raider*.

"Less movie, more nightmare," Jamaal said with a sneer.

"You saw it happen?" she asked with wide eyes.

"No. None of the djinn were present, or we would

have stopped the idiots that cracked the seal and released the demons."

"Idiots as in someone did this intentionally?" Felicia asked sharply.

"They probably didn't know what they were doing. We never had a chance to question them. Those present when the seal to the demon rift was broken all died," Tariq informed.

"If they're dead and you weren't there, how do you know what happened?" Zane asked.

"Because not all of them died that same day," Tariq explained. "Some managed to run away but took ill. The doctors said they succumbed to tomb toxins." The gases of the dead could become potent, especially over time.

"If they suffered from grave poisoning, then their account of events can't be taken seriously. It is a documented fact that the inhalation of those gases can cause strange behavior, including hallucinations and the sensation of voices talking. Perhaps they only thought they released demons." Zane played devil's advocate.

"Are you saying we imagined the demons attacking our people?" Jamaal growled. "Because I did not imagine this." He pointed to the scars slanting across half his face.

"I am not saying you weren't attacked," Zane said, standing firm. "However, you are expecting me to believe that some ancient rift opened and loosed some super demon ghosts on the world. Which seems unlikely. Perhaps they've been here all along."

"And I say they've been imprisoned for eons."

Ella raised her hand. "Um, rather than argue, I can show everyone what really happened."

Everyone blinked at her, except Felicia. "Can you really?"

Pursing her lips, Ella rolled a shoulder. "Guess we'll find out. Can you turn on the television?" Before Felicia could move, one of Ella's eager ghosts had already found the remote and powered it. The painting above the fireplace slid upwards to reveal an LCD screen. It lit and briefly flashed a news channel before flipping inputs to sit on one showing only staticky snow.

Closing her eyes, Ella centered herself. Displaying rather than telling a spirit's experience took more out of her, but it also forestalled questions.

Let everyone see what the ghost showed her.

"Come on, Esfir. Show us through your eyes." *Let me ride along in your memories.*

With an invitation, the female spirit that claimed to have seen it all dove into Ella. There was a brief struggle for control. There always was when spirits suddenly got a chance to wear flesh. But this was no demon. Ella could and did control the ghost. She aimed the esoteric juice she wrung from its memories at the television.

It crackled and flashed, the feedback wince worthy. Then cleared.

The view proved slightly dizzying as they literally saw out of someone else's eyes. Someone high above the ground riding in a helicopter. The view outside the windows was of an arid place, built of hard-packed dirt and rock. A barren, uninhabitable plain suddenly broken by a rift. The helicopter dove into that abyss, deeper than expected. Mountains of sandstone rose in steep cliffs on either side, and while there was distance between the walls of rock, the split appeared fresh.

Those watching couldn't know this, but the ghost whose memories she borrowed remembered the satellite images of three months ago showed no sign of the crevice.

The new gorge didn't go unnoticed. Or unexplored. A camp could be seen on the dusty, rubble-strewn ground. Tents of thick, tan canvas, the kind not easily seen from above by spying eyes, littered the area, hiding in the shadows of the cliffs.

When the helicopter lurched to land, Ella's stomach went with it.

The perspective on screen was that of a first-person shooter type video game. Wobbly as it moved, with no real control of where it turned to focus. For example, Ella wanted to more closely examine the tent with the odd symbol on it, but the person running this movie was more interested in exiting the helicopter and heading toward something on the other side of camp at the base of the mountain where the crack ended.

People spoke, and despite not knowing any language other than English, she knew it to be some Arabic dialect. She understood it, too.

"The satellite eye won't be watching again for

another three hours. Get the helicopter to return to town for supplies." Because they only moved when nobody watched.

"I hear we're having lamb tonight for dinner."

"Let's hope this time he doesn't burn it."

Inane chatter that was left behind as her ghost walked them past the tents to a slit within the rock at the vee where the crevice ended. Within, instant quiet, and cool. The heat of the sun didn't penetrate this far. The slim aperture, less then a pace wide and barely high enough for a person to walk, went on for several minutes. Several minutes where even the sound of huffing breath seemed too loud.

Like the gorge, the rock appeared freshly cut, the edges sharp rather than smoothed by time. A heaving of the very ground itself that unearthed a treasure.

The unnatural muffled quiet ended abruptly, the shadowed passage suddenly emerging into a cavern bright with lights and full of noise.

Ella was among many to gasp as the view on the screen changed. She couldn't help but mutter, "Just like a movie." And by that she meant the temple on the screen. The columns rising several stories, buried inside the mountain itself, almost as if the stone had been grown around it. Every section of the pillars was carved, the symbols intricate, and unreadable thus far.

Unreadable by the spirit whose memories they followed, but not by a really old djinn. "They should have heeded the warnings that were carved," Azzam said, making Ella crease her brow as the voice caused the vision to waver.

"What does it say?" Tariq asked. "I don't recognize some of the symbols."

"I'm gonna guess it says bad shit ahead, don't touch," was Jamaal's sarcastic retort.

It was Felicia who shushed them. "Shut up. I want to know what happens."

The image on screen steadied. Esfir, who was the ghost reliving the moment, turned from the wondrous feat of architecture and magic. She noted a man with a cigarette dangling from his mouth, but unlit in this relic of a place. He held a video camera in his hand. He watched the tiny screen.

"Jacques." The female voice could be heard, not seen, probably because Esfir's body was the avatar riding the memories. "Did you crack the code to get in?" The query emerged, and Jacques turned for a look before shaking his head.

"Nothing yet, *mon amour*. We can't even be sure where the door is. We've gone over every inch of this place and have yet to even find a seam. I hate to say it, but I think we'll have to blow it open."

A shame. A site this old would have pulled in a large sum if dismantled and sold to a collector.

"I figured you might say that. A shipment of charges is scheduled to arrive this afternoon. By tomorrow morning, we'll have a hole and be able to see what's hiding on the other side. By this time next month, we should be rich."

"And vacationing on a beach."

"I already bought the bikini," Esfir said with a titter.

"Here's to hoping there's plenty of treasure behind this wall so we never have to work again, *mon amour*," Jacques stated.

"I see I've arrived just in time." The strange voice drew attention, and Esfir whirled to see a man with a deep tan, slicked dark hair, and a white suit entering the cavern.

"Who are you? You're not allowed to be here," Jacques blustered.

"And neither are you. This is not a safe place for humans." The stranger shook his finger at them, as if chiding a naughty child.

"Don't you mean it's not safe for you?" Jacques pulled the pistol he wore at his hip and fired.

He missed. Somehow, the man in the white suit was no longer at the mouth of the cavern but standing in front of the temple.

How had he moved so quickly?

"You foolish, foolish humans. Do you have any idea what you play with?" The man with his oiled beard and gleaming eyes turned from the glyphs on the columns to regard them sternly. "There is a reason this place was hidden. Did you not heed the warning signs?" He swept a hand, indicating all the intricate carvings.

"It's ours. We found it," Jacques growled. "So step aside before I make you regret it." He aimed his gun.

"Humans and their toys." A snap of the fingers and the gun went from Jacques' grip to the stranger's. He held it aloft and shook his head. "We should have never granted the wish of flaming powder." He flung the gun from him, only it turned into dust, the motes drifting to the ground.

Magic.

Impossible.

Jacques looked as pale as the falling ash. "Who are you?"

"A guardian who is telling you one last time to leave."

"We aren't leaving. It's our treasure. We found it."

"And you will forget it."

Those fingers lifted, and the man went to speak, only to pause as a low, vibrating hum swept the room, trembled the very rocky foundations and sifted silt from the ceiling.

The man in white turned his head to stare at the wall. Placed his hand against it and bowed his head, as if listening.

Jacques raised a second gun that he pulled from an ankle holster.

Bang.

This time, the strange man didn't evade the speeding bullet. A red stain spread across his white suit. He turned back to face Jacques—hand still braced on the glyphs—opened his mouth, and said, "That hurt. It's not supposed to hurt." His brows beetled as if in concentration, and he began to slump, only he didn't fall far. His hand remained stuck to the wall. Literally stuck, and the edge of it glowed.

"I told you to move away," Jacques said, sweat beading his brow, while Esfir stood in shocked silence.

The man in white cursed. "Fucking moron. Do you know what you've done? Quickly. You mustn't let my blood touch the stone."

Or what?

Jacques took the warning as a reason to shoot again.

The bullet went right through the body, spraying the wall with blood. The man in white fell against the temple, gasping for breath. "Stupid human, you've doomed us all."

Words that made no sense. Words that tapered as the life in his eyes faded. One last exhale and his body went limp.

Everything was quiet.

The crack sounded louder than it should have. A dark line appeared in the wall amidst the blood splatter. It zigzagged from that spot moving up, then left and right, a spider crack that webbed. From it seeped a mist, a greenish miasma that quickly brought a rotten smell to the nose. The stench of sulphur caused gagging. Being closest, Jacques' eyes watered as he gasped, "We need to get out of here. It is the death burp."

It truly was. Jacques no sooner spoke than his body arched. His eyes turned a bright, glowing red. He opened his mouth and said, "Freed—" *Splat.*

He exploded into meaty chunks. They hit exposed flesh with hot, wet slaps.

"Jacques!" Esfir screamed his name and yet knew nothing could help him. She had to save herself.

Running back through the crevice, hot wind nipped at the heels, crawled up the spine. Curled around the neck. Crept into the mouth, filling the mind with visions of power. Doom.

Nothingness.

Ella gasped as the memories abruptly halted. The screen went to white snow once more.

Silence permeated the room.

It was Felicia who broke it with a bright, "I don't know about everyone else, but that totally stirred my appetite. Dinner, anyone?"

EIGHT

HER STATEMENT DREW the attention of those present from the brutal carnage on the screen as they stared at her with shocked expressions. Despite her blasé words, truth be told, Felicia also felt a chill.

What kind of power did these demons, just released from their prison, have that they could explode a person, literally? And more important, could they do the same to a vampire?

She wasn't about to volunteer to find out.

Rather than adjourn to the dining room—even though she was, in truth, feeling a bit peckish—they chose to remain in the library. Her human servants filed in quietly to offer beverages and left behind a tray of snacks. For Ella mostly. Humans required regular feeding and sleep, just like any other pet.

Felicia stuck to her infused red wine, joined by Zane. As for the djinn, they huddled in a tight circle. The old one appeared angry. She couldn't hear their conversation no matter how hard she tried. Probably some kind of spell to hide it. But she saw their faces. Jamaal, mocking. Tariq, stern. Whereas Azzam gestured and talked, getting wound up.

Since they were involved in their own drama, she addressed Ella. "Is the demon that came out of the crack and took over Jacques the same one who used you to talk?"

Ella shook her head. "I don't know. Maybe. The memories I funneled were from the ghost's perception, colored by her state of mind at the time."

"She being...?"

"A traitor." The cone of silence dissipated, and Jamaal answered.

"A traitor how?" Felicia asked.

"They did not come across that location by accident," Tariq supplied. "Esfir worked for us."

"And you think she stole the location of the temple from you?" asked Felicia. She kept a close eye on her staff. Cameras kept them honest. As did their blood bond to their queen.

"Stole or saw something she shouldn't have then told her lover. Our own fault in a sense because we've been self-absorbed." Azzam was the one to reply. "Many of the djinn had retreated from the world. Choosing to spend their lives in their bottles. Watching the world rather than participating in it."

"Wait, you really live in bottles?" Ella exclaimed. "Can I see one?"

"No." Tariq's lips pulled into a flat line. "When the demonic essences escaped, they possessed humans—"

"I thought they exploded them."

"Perhaps they did initially, but they soon learned to keep their hosts alive. With bodies to use, and the knowledge they stole from those minds, they went after our sanctuary," Tariq explained.

"Hold on, they attacked you on your home turf?" Zane exclaimed. "Didn't you have safeguards to prevent attacks?"

"We did. However, our protective spells have worn down over time. As Azzam mentioned, we didn't remain vigilant."

"Complacency is the enemy," muttered Felicia.

"Exactly," Tariq agreed. "But even if we were watching, you need to understand the demons are clever. They can hide in plain sight, nestled in a host."

"Like spiritual leeches," Felicia remarked.

"For the moment, and only because their bodies aren't present on this plane. Not yet. Only their essence has managed to escape, and it is but a weak representation of what they can do." This time, Azzam played teacher.

Ella clapped her hands, looking more excited than frightened. "If their plan is to possess humans, then we'll have to foil it."

"And how do you propose to do so?" Tariq asked. "Killing the host only allows the essence to roam once more."

"Who said anything about killing?" Ella squeaked.

"Then how do you propose we fight them?" Jamaal jumped in.

"Holy water and priests, of course." Ella rolled her eyes. "We'll get vats of it. Arm the populace with water guns and crosses."

Tariq grimaced. "If only it were so easy."

"Are you saying we can't exorcise them back to where they came from?" Felicia asked.

"No. Because they are only spirits, which means they can't be killed. Only contained," Azzam stated.

Felicia frowned. "Surely the djinn have the power to handle them?" Judging by the expression on their faces, they couldn't.

"We tried to fight, and failed," Tariq admitted. "The presence of demons renders us vulnerable."

"They're your kryptonite," Ella exclaimed. "When they're around, you can be hurt."

"A modern explanation that actually suits the case." Tariq shook his head. "And it had been so long that we'd forgotten about them. But they didn't forget us. Upon escaping, they began riding humans, making their way to our secret place. Wearing the bodies of our servants, they entered and captured the bottles of my people. Only a few emerged in time to fight. All but Jamaal and Azzam were taken or killed that day."

"And we survived only because you arrived in time to save us." Azzam spread his arms and swung them. "Tariq wielded the mighty thunder hammer of the olden days and did his best to collapse the walls on the demon hosts. But they were many. He wasn't in time to stop one from tearing out part of my magical core." The old man's lips turned down.

Ella looked at him with a frown. "So that's why your soul is bleeding."

"You can see it?" Azzam asked sharply.

"Well, yeah. You and Jamaal are leaking all over the place. I'm surprised you haven't fixed it," Ella said.

"We haven't because we can't. Djinn can't heal other djinn or themselves. Part of the restrictions on our magic," Tariq explained.

"You can't. Can someone else, though?" Felicia asked.

"Who?" Jamaal asked, his lip curled in a sneer. "You? Because I'd rather be human than a flesh-eating leech."

"And I'd rather floss than be your sire," was her sharp retort. Felicia cocked her head. "Ella, you say you can see the damage. Can you do something to help?"

Ella gnawed her lower lip. "Maybe."

It was Azzam who said, "Could you try?"

"I don't know if I can fix it, but I think I can stop the bleed."

"Think?" Tariq bristled. "I don't want my grandfather being part of some experiment by a witch."

"What's the worse the chit can do?" Azzam asked.

"Kill you." Tariq's words hung in the air.

No surprise, Zane took offense. "You don't want her helping, then that's fine by me."

"Zane." Ella put her hand on his arm. "Putting a seal over the holes in their spirits won't hurt me."

"How would you know? You've never done it before. And these are djinn. We don't know how their magic will affect you if you try."

"Only one way to find out." Before anyone could stop her, Ella sprang from her seat on the couch. Her eyes began to glow, shining white, but also swirling with gray. The tips of her hair lifted, and for a moment, a swirl of gray smoke with shapes within it could be seen. Her hands reached out for Azzam and grabbed him despite Tariq's shouted, "No."

When Tariq would have slapped her hands away, a force knocked him back and then pinned him.

The ghosts didn't like anyone manhandling their Ella. As for Felicia, she sat back and watched. This new element of Ella's magic was uncharted and fascinating. Just how much could she do wielding the spirits?

The old man's mouth gaped wide open, and his eyes rolled back in his head. A mist rolled from Ella's mouth, pouring out of her into Azzam, and he appeared to inhale it.

When the fog trailed to a trickle, Ella's mouth snapped shut and she released the man. She took a step back, stumbled, and Zane was there to grab her.

"Goodness, that was a little more intense than expected," she exclaimed before fainting.

Zane swept her into his arms and glared at everyone present. "Are you happy now?"

"Don't be such an ogre," Felicia remarked. "She fainted. It happens. Take her to her chambers." A set of rooms reserved for Ella and Zane for the times they stayed over. "I am sure she'll wake shortly."

Without replying, Zane left. Tariq rose to his feet, brushing himself off as he strode to his grandfather who stood with a bemused look on his face.

"Azzam, speak to me. What did the witch do to you?"

"She's not a witch!" Felicia took offense.

He turned his agitated gaze on her. "Witch, sorceress, it is only a word. I want to know what she's done."

The old man turned to face him, and Felicia was stunned to see tears in his eyes. "She did it. She stopped my magic from leaking."

Further questioning, though, revealed that she'd only managed to stem the bleed. The missing chunk was still gone. Azzam's access to his magic remained very limited. But it was more than he'd had a few hours before. It caused a wistful hope in Jamaal.

"Think her vampire husband will allow her to do the same for me?" he asked.

"He won't have a choice," Tariq declared imperiously.

Whereas Felicia knew Zane would require convincing if Ella showed any ill effects. "I think the more important thing to note is the fact we can do something."

"Too little too late. The demons have already struck and won against my kind. Their victory with the djinn is just the beginning."

"What do you mean?"

Azzam stroked his beard. "They managed to defeat us using humans. Let that sink in. Humans took down the most powerful users of magic. And those spirits are a result of a simple crack in the seal holding them prisoner. Once the wall that holds the rift shut fully tumbles down, we won't have their weaker spirits attacking us. We shall be overrun by the legions lying in wait."

"Legions?"

"Thousands of demons, in all their horrid glory and murderous intent, shall spill onto the land. If that happens, we are all doomed."

NINE

AFTER AZZAM'S GRIM ANNOUNCEMENT, the vampire queen left them to check on Ella. Tariq took that time to settle his tired grandfather in a suite allocated to them by the human staff. A staff he kept an eye on. He knew how easily humans could be turned.

The queen's assurance that they were loyal to her didn't assuage his concern. Their servants had been loyal to them, too, and look what happened.

Leaving his suite of rooms, he ran into Jamaal.

"Where are you going?" his brother asked.

"To talk with the queen. I want to know more about her witch."

"Is it wise for us to separate?"

"Do you really think we're any safer together?" Tariq arched a brow.

But Jamaal paced, his brow creased in worry. "We aren't safe anywhere. They know we are here. They will come for us."

"Which is why I strengthened the wards on this house and the grounds. Unlike our home, we will not be taken unaware."

"If they're not already here. You heard the demon speak through the girl."

"Speak, yes," Tariq admitted, "but not act, leading me to believe that her ability to command the spirits allocates her some protection."

"Does it?"

"Why are you determined to hate her?" Tariq asked, only to immediately gain the insight on why. "You're afraid she won't be able to heal you like she healed Azzam."

"You heard her mate. He doesn't want her to do it again. And what if she can't?"

"She will, and if her mate disagrees, then I'll deal with it." See how the vampire male liked being sent to the Antarctic with no one to suck on but penguins and seals.

"Even if she can plug the hole in me, what good does it do? It's only a matter of time before the demons spill into his world and we're all dead."

"Meaning?"

"Why bother? Why not just have as much fun as we can?"

Because not bothering was what had led them to this in the first place. Complacency was their enemy. They'd spent so long doing their own thing—rarely interacting with the outside world—that they lost sight of themselves. Of everything.

Tariq was one of the few in the last decade to emerge from his glass shell only to realize how much everything had changed. The world held a lot less magic than before. Industrialization had killed off giant swaths of it. Cities were especially bad. Their energy lines disrupted by blasting and construction.

No wonder the ancient spells they'd taken for granted failed. Things would have been much different for his brethren had they not been taken by surprise.

"Have you wondered why they took the bottles?" Not only taken them but stoppered them. Because while it didn't take a rub to get a djinn out of his safe place, they could be imprisoned with a magical cork.

"To smash them for fun? Who knows why those murderous creatures felt a need to attack us," Jamaal said.

But Tariq had a feeling the why was important. If it were simply about killing the djinn, then why not smash the bottle right away to release them? The djinn were mortal in the presence of demons, and none of them remembered how to fight. They would have been easy to slaughter. But the demons chose to steal the bottles with the djinn inside instead. Why?

And why did they chase after Tariq and his family still? What did the demons want?

"I'm going to speak to the queen."

"Sure, you are." Jamaal rolled his eyes. "Not that I blame you. I'm tempted to try for a piece of that ass myself."

Tariq's fist shot out before he even realized he'd drawn it back.

It earned him a glare from Jamaal as he rubbed his jaw. "What was that for?"

"Watch your mouth when you speak of her. She is our hostess, not a common whore."

"She is a blood sucker. A leech."

"A woman with intelligence and character. And who are you to call her leech? Are we not the same?"

"We don't feed off people."

"No, but we do feed from everything else around us." Djinn were creatures of magic, and magic was all around. Just the act of breathing in air fed them.

"We are not the same," Jamaal insisted.

"You keep telling yourself that and you keep pretending you can't fight. Me, I'm not giving in without an attempt. Maybe you want the world to end, but I've discovered I'm not ready for that yet." Not ready to stop living. Especially now that he'd found a woman who intrigued and drew him.

The wards at her bedroom door didn't stop him. He entered her pink sanctum to discover she wasn't in her room, but rather outside on her rooftop deck. She sat on a cushioned bench, staring at the stars and didn't startle at his approach.

"Perhaps you were in your bottle too long to remember, but it's considered common courtesy to knock," she said without turning around.

"I wanted to see you."

"And you considered that cause enough to barge into my room. Again."

"Admit it, you're happy to see me." She might not have the heat of a human infusing her veins, but even a vampire had tells. The way she forgot to breathe. Her hands too calmly folded in her lap. The stillness of her frame.

"Why are you here?"

"How is Ella?"

"Fine. She's already awake and basking in the overbearing attention of her mate. Really quite disgusting the way he coddles her."

"He loves her." An emotion Tariq had studied and understood in essence. He loved his brother, his grandfather. But they were family. He'd never loved a woman. Enjoyed? Yes. However, none ever had the power to engage him for long.

Until now.

"Zane's affection makes him weak."

"I doubt he'd agree."

Felicia sighed. "Because he's a fool."

"A fool who is your friend." Another thing he didn't have. Tariq had spent much of his life observing the world. Learning about it. Sleeping for decades out of sheer boredom.

"He and Ella are both friends, which is why I'm pretty sure I'm going to regret having agreed to let you and your family visit."

"The demons are coming regardless of our presence." Although the djinn being in her home might hasten it.

"Much as I hate to admit it, I know you're right. That they'll come no matter what. Doesn't mean I can't blame you." Her smirk in his direction brought an answering smile.

"Rather than blame, we need to create a plan."

"What kind of plan?" She spread her hands. "You said it yourself. We kill the host; the spirit moves to another. You can't fight them without exposing yourself."

"And yet, a long time ago, we managed to conquer them and seal them away from this world."

"Do you know how they did that?" she asked.

He shook his head. "No. The knowledge of it remains hidden for the moment. But I've been searching. I think your soul sorceress is the key."

"I wouldn't doubt it. Ella is special. Exactly what do you think she has to do with all this?"

He shrugged. "My research thus far hasn't born fruit."

"If you do find something, let me know."

"Speaking of Ella, I am pleased to hear the witch has recovered. Jamaal is worried Ella won't heal him like she did Azzam."

"I am sure if she can, she will. Idiot girl likes to help people." Said with disdain.

"You say 'help' like it's a bad thing."

"Because she has no sense of self-preservation.

She's too nice. Has yet to learn helping others weakens you."

"An odd comment for a queen. Surely you aid your subjects."

"My subjects help themselves. I merely keep them in line. Surely you have a king or something that does the same." She cast him a querying glance.

"No king or emperor. No one to govern us at all. We are a solitary people. Once we stopped being slaves to the wishes of humans, we withdrew. Pursued our own interests. We didn't need someone to rule us. Merely caretakers to ensure we weren't disturbed."

"Sounds...lonely."

For a long time, he didn't think so. In all his centuries, Tariq had many sexual partners because djinn did enjoy the pleasures of the flesh, but he'd never found a mate. Never wanted to.

He couldn't imagine getting stuck with one person for the length of his existence. Because mating, a real mating with a djinn, wasn't something done lightly. It bound them together, forever.

Appalling really. Didn't it get boring being with one entity for life?

Isn't being alone just as boring? He glanced over at the vampire queen. Her face turned away, giving him her profile. The sleek tilt of her nose, the fine line of her jaw.

Beautiful, and yet, it was when she spoke that his mind truly engaged. He felt...*alive*.

A strange sensation he didn't understand.

"Any ideas on what we should do about the demons?" she asked.

"I'm not sure if we can do anything." Something he hated to admit because it sounded hopeless. "You heard Azzam. It took a coven to seal the breach the last time it happened, yet by Ella's own account, she is the only soul sorceress in existence. She won't have the power to do it alone."

"But you said it yourself, it's only a crack."

"A crack that could shatter at any moment."

"Then why hasn't it?" Felicia mused aloud. "There must be something missing. Something they're waiting for to bust out of their prison."

"An interesting observation." As well as something Tariq himself wondered about. Did this have something to do with the bottles they'd stolen?

"I'll have Ella ask her ghost friends about it. Perhaps they know something." The queen went silent, and yet he wasn't ready to leave.

"I don't believe I've thanked you yet for granting us succour in your home."

"Don't thank me. I was curious. Your kind aren't exactly common."

"So you think me interesting?"

Her gaze met his, and coyness curved her lips. "Maybe."

He leaned closer. "I've not had much interaction with your kind either. I find you"—*Sexy. Desirable*—"fascinating."

She stood and took a few paces, putting distance between them. "We are very different."

"Are we?" He heard her startled breath as he moved quickly, placing himself at her back, his words whispering on the nape of her neck, exposed by the hair she'd pulled into a messy chignon.

"What are you doing?" She whirled to face him.

"Isn't it obvious?" He smiled. "You are very attractive."

"I'm a queen."

"Even queens have lovers."

"Is that what you want us to be, lovers?" She arched a fine brow.

"Yes." No point in being subtle. Who knew how much time they'd have together. "I think we would find much pleasure together."

"You might be right."

"I know I am."

Her lips quirked. "Let's say I agreed. Our involvement wouldn't mean I'd help you indefinitely. If I think you and your family pose a danger to my brethren, I will toss you to the demons myself."

"I wouldn't expect you to do any less. *My queen.*" He couldn't help but add a low rumble to the words as his hand curled around the indent of her waist and drew her near.

Her gaze remained intent on his, her lips parted. "This is probably a bad idea."

"I think it's a worse one if we don't explore it." He dipped his head and claimed her mouth.

A jolt went through him, a shock much like the first time they'd kissed. But this time, he didn't intend to make it brief.

He slanted his mouth over hers, testing its softness. Her body curved into his, a melding that would have been much nicer with no clothes. But he didn't dare move too fast with this woman.

The tip of his tongue teased the seam of her lips, and she parted them wide enough for him to taste her. To mingle their bodily essences in a way that brought awareness to his skin.

A tingle to his loins.

A glow to his very soul.

He lifted her off the ground, wrapping her in his arms, bringing her to his level that he might fully enjoy the kiss. Her arms laced around his neck, hugging him tight.

There was a sense of rightness in their touch. An explosive need with each embrace. Despite the clothes keeping them apart, his senses were aroused. He took simple pleasure in the way she opened her mouth to him, tasted him.

He began to walk with her back toward the bedroom, only to halt as they both detected a presence. They broke the embrace, and he instinctively tucked the queen behind him, bulking himself up with magical armor against an attack.

Only there was no demon or hordes of humans with torches. Just a petite blonde wearing a man's shirt.

Ella's eyes shone with ethereal light. Her words

held a haunting otherworldly quality. "Upon the rising of the third night of the blood moon, and the sacrifice of magic, the seal shall break, and the legions will be free to feed upon mankind."

"Ella." Felicia slipped out of his protective shadow and headed cautiously to her friend. "What are you doing here? Where's Zane?"

Shaking her head as if coming out of a trance, Ella smiled. "Sorry about that. The ghosts had a message to give you and insisted I tell you right away."

"You said something of the third night of the blood moon?"

"Which doesn't exist. Blood moons are a one-day thing. Two at the most. I've never heard of it happening three nights in a row," Tariq remarked.

"Because it's rare, silly." Ella rolled her eyes. "But it's coming, and we need to get to the crack before it comes to seal it."

"You mean we still have time?" Hope fluttered where before despair had taken root.

"Yes. So no more smooching. Get packing because we need to go on a road trip!"

TEN

"I FORBID IT!" Zane announced, trying to end the conversation.

Ella ignored him and kept packing. Out of Felicia's closet. Zane still wouldn't let them go home. Ever since the shooting, he'd become quite irrational. Convinced of danger at every turn. The only reason they'd even left the hotel was because the poltergeists around Ella began to draw attention.

They were agitated. Even now, they swirled chaotically. Urging haste. Begging her to hide. Cackling the end was nigh.

"Run and hide, like a little mouse, before the hawks eat you."

"The prince of darkness comes, and humans will feed his legions."

"You can still stop the end of the world." The one ghostly voice she chose to listen to.

Even her husband couldn't sway her otherwise.

"You can forbid it all you like, but I am going. Are you coming, too?" Her husband might try to boss her around, and sometimes Ella allowed it. But, at the same time, Ella wasn't that fragile little girl he'd rescued from the asylum anymore. She could protect herself. She could protect others. And she wasn't about to let the world end because her husband was afraid.

"Moonbeam." He groaned her name. "You're talking about traveling to the Middle East. Do you have any idea how far that is?"

"Far. Which is why we're flying." Which Azzam declared was dangerous. However, they didn't have time to waste. The blood moon fast approached.

"Why must you vex me?"

"Because, if I didn't, you might not love me."

"He only loves you for your blood."

"Vampires don't love."

"You—"

He wrapped his arms around her and lifted her off her feet, silencing the ghosts. Only his touch could do that. "I love you more than anything. Nothing will ever change that."

"I know, which is why you'll come with me to be my shield as I battle the legions of darkness."

He groaned. "This is not a movie, Ella."

"I am aware of that. It's more exciting than a movie, and more important, too." She cupped his cheeks. "I have to do this, Zane. I'm the only one who can stop it."

"I hate that you're so good."

"I know, and believe me, if it weren't a matter of

the world ending, I wouldn't make you go. I know how much you hate the desert and the heat."

"Just so you know, I refuse to wear shorts."

"Are you sure? You might get uncomfortably warm."

He glared. She grinned. The thought of her properly attired husband in khaki shorts showing off his glaringly white legs was funny.

"You do realize we'll be vulnerable in the daytime when Felicia and I must hide."

"So we'll travel at night. No different than what we do now." Only rarely did Zane go out in the day. Covered head to toe, face behind a balaclava, eyes shielded with sunglasses.

"If the djinn keeps annoying me, I might eat him."

"If he keeps doing it on purpose, I'll let you." Because no doubt Tariq would keep nudging. The man didn't seem to grasp that Zane wasn't a human he could push around. What she did find interesting was the fact Felicia seemed to like the guy.

"Do you have any idea what we're supposed to do once we find this temple?"

She shrugged. "Kill the mummy."

"It's demons we're facing, not reanimated corpses."

"I'm sure we'll figure it out once we get there."

His lips flatlined. "In other words, you're planning to talk to any lingering ghosts. You're only one soul sorceress, moonbeam. You heard what Azzam said. It took thirteen last time."

"Thirteen to close a hole. This is just a crack."

"Has it occurred to you that getting too close to that crack will allow the demons an easier time possessing you?"

"They can't control me."

"They've spoken through you twice."

"Because I've allowed it. Think of it as me being a receiver for their message."

"How about not being anything for them?"

She stomped her foot. "I'm doing this."

"Not if I tie you to a bed," he grumbled.

"That's for later once we save the world." She winked as she zipped her suitcase shut. "Right now, we've got a plane to catch."

A plane that Azzam refused to board. They stood on the tarmac, the plane at their back, fueled and ready to go. Except someone refused to cooperate.

"No. It's not safe. Man wasn't meant to fly in mechanical coffins." Azzam shook his head.

"We don't have time to do it your way again, Grandfather. We must reach the temple before the blood moon." Tariq kept his cool, but he couldn't prevent the tic at his temple.

"You won't reach the temple at all if you insist on flying in that death trap." Azzam glared at the private jet.

"Your magic isn't recovered enough to transport yourself, and you know I can't bring you and Jamaal. Or is this your way of saying I should leave you behind? I'm sure I can handle a pair of vampires and a witch."

"We have to fly because *no one* can teleport," Ella piped in. "The spirits are claiming the demons have blocked off that route."

"Your ghosts are mistaken," was Tariq's haughty reply.

"Really?" She smirked. "Prove it. Go to Paris and bring me back a fresh croissant."

"If you insist." Tariq nodded. Folded his arms. Stood still. Frowned. Shifted his weight. Frowned some more.

Whereas Ella's grin widened. "Told you. The demons have cast some kind of spell preventing it. Which means..." She cast an eye on the plane.

Azzam protested some more, whereupon Jamaal sighed. "Someone get ready to catch him." Jamaal clubbed Azzam on the back of the head, sending his grandfather down in a forced nap. Tariq nabbed him before he hit the pavement.

"Was that necessary?" he snapped at his brother.

"Yes." Jamaal didn't look one bit repentant.

"If we're done, can we get going? The sun won't stay down forever." The fact that they even managed to get organized enough to leave that same night was impressive. The power of money, Zane called it.

Felicia made a few calls. Greased a few palms. And now, they were on their way on the luxury jet.

With a room that held a bed!

Which Ella immediately claimed.

ELEVEN

WITH THE BEDROOM commandeered by a lusty witch and her vampire, that left the rest of them in the main body of the plane. Azzam was strapped to the couch, which flipped into a bed. Jamaal chose to sit in the cockpit with the pilot just in case he got possessed, leaving Tariq and Felicia more or less alone.

He arched a brow and leaned back in clear invitation. His lap did tempt, but now wasn't the time or place.

She sat primly across from him, tablet held high as she read something way less interesting than his dirty mind. They spent a few hours of flight thus, until finally she cracked and spoke first.

"There's been some thefts of artifacts from museums and private collections in the last few weeks."

"And I care about robberies in the human world because?"

"Because these thefts all seem to have one thing in common. Magic."

That drew his attention. "How do you know that?"

She flipped her tablet to show him. "That scepter, stolen from the London Museum, belonged to a queen who practiced magic." She swiped her finger across the screen and changed the view. "That ring and the goblet stolen here also had—"

"Magic." He frowned. "Do we know for sure it's the demons?"

She shrugged. "Hard to tell. The articles don't say much other than the perpetrators were violent in their intent, didn't bother to hide at all from the cameras, and refused to surrender when police caught up to them." The carnage had the trademarks of a demon assault.

"So the attack on the djinn might be related to this collection of magic."

"I'd say it's most likely."

"And we still don't know why. I've pulled information from every known library in the world, and it hasn't yielded much usable information." He sighed. "Are we being foolish? Should we have found a position to reinforce as Jamaal suggested?"

She snorted. "Hide like animals? I'd rather die fighting."

He couldn't help but smile at her vehemence. "If only the djinn had your spirit."

"You do. I heard what Azzam said; you fought."

"Not very well, apparently. They still stole my people and hurt my family."

"But you tried at least, which is more than most would do. It's noble."

Noble? The very idea warmed even as his failure returned to haunt him. "It accomplished nothing."

"You're alive."

"Am I? There are times I wonder."

For some reason, his words resonated with her. How many times had she thought about dying for a purpose? She, too, had lived a long time and wondered what the point was. Sometimes the loneliness of it overwhelmed.

She stood, crossed the space between them, and sat in his lap.

He couldn't have look more surprised if he tried. "What—"

"Shhh." She placed a finger on his lips. "We don't want to wake Azzam."

The corners of his eyes crinkled, and rather than reply, he kissed her.

It proved as electric as before. And she didn't understand it. She'd kissed many men in her life. Women, too. None, not a single one, ever made her feel so alive. Real. Even better, he wanted nothing from her. Not eternal life, nor a spot in her court.

He had his own power. His own riches. And yes, while he came to her for help, he did so because of a grave danger. Because of his warning, they might have a chance.

But that wasn't why she sat in his lap and kissed him back. She wanted Tariq. Plain and simple.

Wanted to taste his mouth and that spicy ambrosia that was uniquely his. Wanted to touch the smoothness of this tanned skin. To feel him inside of her.

Yet, once again, they were interrupted.

Something in the air changed. A subtle shift in the pressure that sent Tariq to his feet and Felicia scrambling to hers. Her nose twitched, but it was Ella, looking rumpled and pink-cheeked, emerging from the bedroom, yelling, "Jamaal, watch out!" who gave the warning.

"Jamaal!" Tariq bolted for the cockpit, yelling his brother's name. The door remained shut in front of him, and no amount of pounding opened it. His magic fought against the force sealing it. Meanwhile, he could hear scuffling beyond it. Thumps and grunts of a fight.

"Out of the way," Ella ordered. She held out her hand, and he could see the spirits, almost gleeful in their haste, rushing for the door and through it.

Splat. The wet explosion made more noise than expected, especially when accompanied by Jamaal yelling, "Gross. Seriously. Who the fuck explodes a human?"

Demons exploded humans, and who better to blow up than their pilot?

The door sprang open as their plane immediately began to dip, sending those standing staggering. Felicia calmly seated herself even though inside she was slightly disturbed. For one, it was daylight outside.

Two, they were over the ocean, no land in sight, and three...

Three, she had no brilliant plan to deal with this, but she did know panicking wouldn't help.

"Anyone know how to fly a plane?"

Tariq stuck his head into the cockpit and grumbled. "There are body chunks everywhere," he announced. "They're gumming up the electronics."

"Then clean it."

"I can remove the remains"—he snapped his fingers and removed the lovely smell of fresh blood—"but I'm not an engineer. I don't know how to fix what shorted."

"You're a djinn. Djinn can do anything."

"Within reason. We use magic to move stuff. To bring us items. To influence. But there are limits to what we can do. Repair?" He shrugged. "Unless we have intimate knowledge of what we're doing, then it's like handing a hammer to a child."

"Can't you snap your fingers and magic a new plane dashboard?"

"It's not that simple. Given time, maybe I could, but we don't have time."

"We need to abandon ship," Ella stated. "Women and children first."

"Um, Ella. This isn't a boat. We can't just open a door and jump out," Felicia remarked.

Zane appeared from the back, looking like a ninja wearing black from head to toe, including goggles. He tossed a package at Felicia. "You might want to put on your emergency suit."

"I'm less worried about baking in the sun than I am crashing into the ocean. I don't swim." Felicia grumbled, digging through her bag for her gear.

"No one is swimming," Tariq announced. "What is a plane but a giant carpet?"

Felicia eyed him. "You have enough magic to keep it aloft?"

"No. Which is why we're going to float."

More than a few pairs of eyes blinked at him, but it was Felicia who remarked, "We'll sink."

"Not if I protect us. I'll plug any holes with magic and buoy us."

"So you're planning to what? Paddle us to shore? How many months will that take?" was her sarcastic rejoinder.

"It won't take that long. I have a plan, but I need everyone to strap in. This might get bumpy."

Ella plopped herself into a seat, Zane right beside her. Azzam still snored. Jamaal eschewed the seats and headed for the back. "I'm going to wash up."

A waste of blood, Felicia personally thought. But she didn't think offering to lick his skin clean would go over well—especially with Tariq.

He took his brother's place in the cockpit, but she couldn't join him. Not with the sun shining so brightly outside and streaming in. But it bothered her she couldn't. Sitting in the cabin, the shades drawn over the windows, none of them could see the danger coming. The inevitable crash as the plane plummeted.

Perhaps it was better this way.

Better to die drowning and eaten by fish? An ignoble end to her life.

Why did she assume Tariq would fail? Because what he proposed...that was pure magic. Real magic, and she wasn't sure she trusted it. Which might seem odd. She was, after all, the vampire queen, and yet there was nothing magical about her kind.

Vampirism was a virus that mutated the genes of those infected, changing their biological makeup and forcing them to adopt an entirely new diet. Elves? Pointy-eared humans who could craft things of beauty. Demons were big, ugly brutes. Although, apparently the ones she'd met before were but simpletons compared to the true thing. Mermaids were aquatic creatures, half woman, half fish, and they didn't grow legs.

Even Ella didn't truly have magic. She manipulated souls to do what she needed.

But Tariq? He actually had control of forces she couldn't see or touch or explain. It fascinated. It frightened.

Especially since she had to trust him.

The pitch of the plane grew steep, the nose dipping, and her nails dug into the soft leather armrests. Who cared if she left marks? She'd sacrifice the entire plane to live.

No one said anything as they went into a nosedive. Although Ella did hum.

Only once the melody began repeating in her head

did Felicia snort. "*Ground Control to Major Tom?* Seriously?"

Ella turned her gray gaze on her. "Would you prefer I sing *Plane Crash in C*?"

"How about asking your ghostly friends for some help?"

"I did."

"And?"

"They said not to worry."

Which didn't reassure. Ella had said it more than once. The dead didn't care about the living.

The plane began to shudder, and her fingers dug deeper, ripping into the seat. She hated showing weakness. But at least she wasn't alone. Azzam still snored, strapped to a seat, while Zane leaned back, striving for insouciance. She could see the hard edge in his gaze, the grimness of his jaw.

A noise at the back of the plane showed Jamaal rejoining them, his face wet and his hair slicked back. The blood on his skin was gone, leaving only blotches on his shirt and pants.

He slammed himself into an empty seat.

"Aren't you going to help your brother?" she asked.

"Can't. Broken, remember?" He held up his hands and shrugged.

Ella exclaimed, "Give me a second and I'll fix you."

"Ella, get your ass back in that seat," Zane barked.

As if she'd listen. The ghosts aided her in undoing the buckle and flinging herself across to kneel in front of Jamaal.

He looked nervous, more nervous than Felicia had seen him thus far. But it was pure mischief that lit his gaze when Ella braced her hands on his thighs and he said, "A little bit higher…"

Zane growled.

Ella ignored them all, her head tilting back. Felicia concentrated on the souls swirling around her friend and the mist flowing from her mouth, anything to ignore the fact they were going down.

Jamaal's eyes and mouth were wide as the smoky substance entered him. The stream of mist ended, and he lunged to grab Ella before she keeled over.

Only to have Zane snarl, "Hands off, magic boy," as he reached for his wife.

And then everyone went tumbling, except for Felicia, who'd smartly strapped her seatbelt before the plane hit the water.

TWELVE

THE LANDING WASN'T as soft as he would have liked, but that was because Tariq was saving his magic for other things. Like the bubble he had to immediately encase the plane in. This vessel wasn't an airtight submarine. It would sink if he didn't find a way to keep the water out.

This wasn't the first time he'd done something like this; however, a plane was a big object. Bigger than the last time he'd used this trick. As a boy he'd wanted to find Atlantis, so he'd enchanted a small boat and taken it under water since his father wouldn't teach him how to breathe liquid.

He'd almost drowned that day, going deeper than he should have then getting trapped by a baby leviathan that decided to keep the djinn toy it found bobbing in its playroom.

A good thing Grandfather came looking.

This time, there would be no rescue. Tariq held all

their lives in his hands. He couldn't afford to make a mistake. Yet he already had by not listening to his grandfather. He'd warned them not to fly.

Then again, they hadn't had a choice. A plane over the ocean was the fastest method of travel.

Was.

Now that they'd crashed, how would they get there in time? Felicia had pointed out the problem, and he'd lied. He had no idea how to get them to shore in time to stop the end of the world. He could conjure a fleet of outboard motors, but they wouldn't be fast enough. No boat in existence could travel hundreds of miles in mere hours.

There was no knock, just a sudden opening of the door, quickly shut, and then Ella plopping into the seat beside him.

"Why haven't you called him?"

"Called who?" he asked with puzzlement.

"Your friend down there." She pointed to the waters.

"I have no fish friends," he retorted. Unless the ones on his plate counted.

"Not a fish." She giggled. "The sea monster. The big one you used to play with as a kid."

He blinked. "How did you know about Levi?" Only to answer his own question. "The ghosts, of course." After that first incident with the leviathan, he'd only stayed away a short while. He'd returned time and again to hang with the sea monster, bringing him presents. However, he'd not seen Levi in centuries.

Given humanity's encroachment and pollution, he assumed his friend was dead or hiding in the deep where it was safe.

"Aren't you going to call him?"

"Even if he's still alive, I don't see how he can help us."

"He's not a baby sea monster anymore."

"And I still don't see what you think he can do to help."

"Did you never read any stories about Poseidon and his chariot drawn by seahorses? I don't think I've ever actually heard of sea horses big enough to help us, but wouldn't a leviathan have the strength and speed? Make him your horse."

He gaped at her.

Ella smiled. "You're welcome." With that, she left as rapidly as she'd come. But he paid little mind. He now knew what to do.

First, though, he required something to make a harness. He expended magic conjuring some thick marine rope, then some more fashioning it into a loop that he had to tie around the plane, all while maintaining the bubble's integrity. It left him in a bit of a sweat.

Next, a call to his old friend.

After that first time his grandfather saved him, Tariq, being somewhat stubborn and single-minded, had returned more than once to play with Levi, but in order to ensure no one knew, he taught himself how to fashion gills so he could stay underwater. He even taught himself to web his feet and toes to help him swim. Not that he swam much. His thing as a young lad was to grab Levi around the neck, and then they raced through the warm waves. A sea monster and his boy.

He got the thrill of the ride while Levi got to show off his unique pet, making him the envy of all the other sea monsters.

However, would the leviathan remember him? It had been decades since he'd even thought of Levi.

Yet Ella seemed to think he simply had to call. Could it be that easy? While he'd fabricated the harness, twilight fell, and as if vampires had a sixth sense for it, the door opened, and Felicia entered. She sat in the seat Ella had vacated.

"What's the plan, oh mighty djinn?"

"You probably don't want to know."

"That bad?"

"Would you feel more reassured if I told you Ella suggested it?"

Felicia cocked her head. "Actually, I am."

"She told me to ask a sea monster to pull us to shore."

The vampire queen took a moment to digest this. "And you're hesitating because?"

"There's a chance if I call the wrong one, you and your friends will get crushed and killed."

She glanced at him. "You could snap your fingers and be on shore this minute, couldn't you?"

"Usually, yes, but not in this instance. Teleportation isn't working at the moment."

"But you could save yourself easily. Fly another chair out of here or something."

"Yes. However, I'm not interested in only saving myself."

"For a djinn who isn't supposed to care, you're awfully concerned about others."

"A failing of mine."

Her lips curved. "I've had that problem a time or two of late, too."

He scrubbed his face. "Things were easier when I hung out in my bottle."

"But boring, I'll wager."

He offered a rueful grin. "True. However, at this point, I could do with a little less excitement."

"And once we win this battle, you'll get that wish. So what are you waiting for? Get us to shore."

"I'm waiting for a sign from the gods that this isn't a mistake."

She leaned over and brushed her lips over his. "How's that for a sign?"

"Seems kind of weak."

She laughed. "Fine. How about, if we make it to shore alive, I kiss you somewhere more interesting." Her gaze flicked down to the bulge in his pants. It stirred his simmering hunger.

It gave him incentive. He straightened in his seat. "Now that's what I call a bargain. Time to call a sea monster." He closed his eyes and sent out a call. Not with words. But with waves. He projected his need into the water, sent it flying over currents, hoping Levi would hear it.

He did it for a few hours, Felicia by his side, holding his hand as he called. Offering him support even though he didn't need or ask for it. He did appreciate it, though.

His grandfather, and even Jamaal, had joined him for a spell, but their magical reserves were low. The healing had only stopped the bleed, not replenished it.

Fatigue eventually had him stopping. If that didn't bring Levi—or something else—then nothing would.

He leaned back wearily in his seat.

"You're tired," she observed.

"Depleted. Not much magic around here." Water tended to disrupt it.

"Any way I can help?"

He cast her a glance. "You already are." He squeezed her fingers.

The plane rocked, and Felicia squeaked.

He sensed more than saw the hump heaving out of the water. However, the question was, did he have the right monster?

"I have to go outside."

"But..."

Before he could change his mind, he flung himself at the windshield, dissolving it long enough for his body to pass through then resealing it. Next, he formed his gills, one on each side of his neck, before diving off the nose of the plane and into the water.

Only then did he send out a new thought. *Levi, is that you?*

He sure as hell hoped so when that single eye opened and stared at him from over a gaping maw lined in teeth.

THIRTEEN

FELICIA WATCHED Tariq go into the water and worried. She might have encouraged him to go along with Ella's suggestion because they had no other choice, but that didn't mean she had all the confidence it would work.

A sea monster as a pet?

"I know. I'm jealous, too." Felicia knew better than to be startled when Ella appeared at her elbow and seemed to read her thoughts.

"Are you sure this is the right course of action?"

"It's that, or we bob like a cork and miss the end of the world," Ella stated.

"Expecting a leviathan to drag us to shore is nuts."

"Think of it as epic. It will be great for the book I'm gonna write."

"You're writing a book?"

"Not yet, but I'm going to. *The Adventures of Ella.*" She struck a pose.

"That's crazy," Felicia retorted.

At that, Ella snickered. "Crazy was the story of my falling in love with Zane. The next one will be about how we save the world."

"Which is even crazier."

"Why yes, yes, it is." Ella beamed. "Thank you."

"For what?" she asked, but Ella was gone, and Felicia remained, staring out the cockpit window at the dark, rolling waves.

Waves that suddenly churned, sending the plane bobbing wildly. She grabbed hold of the armrests and held on. Jamaal, staggering into the cockpit, cursed as he slammed around. "What's happening?"

"I think we're about to find out if your brother's plan succeeded."

In another moment, they saw proof it had when the head of the beast emerged, Tariq standing atop it. She noted his wave and then his pointing. She looked down to see the rope he'd fashioned into a harness strung around the neck of the monster.

Then she was yelling as the leviathan took off. Jamaal went tumbling back, and she was glad she'd remained in her seat because they were traveling too fast to stand. Planes might count speed in G-force, but this was sea monster speed, and it sluiced through the waters so fast the plane was airborne, like a kite pulled behind someone running with it.

But it worked.

A few hours later, and before dawn could crest, they came within sight of land.

Only then did the beast stop its mad swim. She was too busy trying to not vomit—which was undignified for a vampire who didn't eat—to notice the monster leaving, but she did sense when Tariq was on board once more. His scent gave it away.

"You did it!" she exclaimed, happier than she should be to see him.

"Did what?" grumbled Azzam, appearing in the cockpit. He took a look around before declaring, "I warned you what would happen if we flew."

"I handled it," Tariq said in his defense.

"By crashing. In the water. Great job." Azzam snorted before leaving again.

"You did good," she reassured, placing a hand on his.

"He is right. We're not safe yet. We need to get off this plane. Prepare to abandon it," he announced.

"But we're still at sea."

"I've called us a boat."

Less called than commandeered, it turned out. It seemed some pirates in these waters noticed the bobbing plane and came to investigate. Felicia and Zane, feeling peckish, took care of the crew and then used the boat to complete the short distance left to shore.

Dear sweet land. She might never leave it again.

Bedraggled didn't describe their state when they finally arrived; however, no one complained. They lived only because of Tariq. The poor man looked utterly exhausted. The planes of his face sharp with fatigue. A fine tremor noticeable in his hands. While he didn't have enough magic to even give them all a fresh outfit, he'd gotten them to shore alive. Which meant he could rest because, on land, Felicia had her power again. The power of money.

In short order, they'd been bustled to a luxury hotel in the heart of Casablanca. A massive four-bedroom suite that housed their whole party.

Ella and Zane got their own room, farthest from everyone else because when those two got busy, the poltergeists went nuts.

That left three rooms. As queen, Felicia took the master.

Azzam took the third bedroom.

She assumed the brothers would bunk together. After all, their bedroom did have two beds. She assumed wrong.

Tariq entered her room, the aroma of him teasing her.

Whirling, her shirt and slacks already on the floor, she wore only the thinnest of lingerie. He might have been tired, but he noticed. His eyes glowed.

"Did you need something?" she asked, breathless.

"Yes." Only the one word, but he advanced on her, his movements slow, almost predatory.

How exciting...

She deliberately said, "You're probably wondering about our next step. I've got a local contact." Abd al Jabbar, the leader of the small coven in this city. "He's arranging vehicles, supplies, and a guide to take us to the coordinates of the temple."

"Don't care." He prowled closer, entering her space. The heat of him rolled off in waves, and she basked in the warmth.

A languorous feeling spread through her. "We should remain vigilant."

"We will. We also need to recover." He ran a knuckle down the side of her face, and she shivered.

"I was going to have a shower then get some sleep."

"Shower, yes. But there's something else we have to do before sleep." The words purred from him softly.

Another shiver trembled her frame. "What would that be?"

His lips curved into a slow, sexy smile. "Don't you owe me something?"

"You're right. I did promise you a kiss." She leaned up and brushed her mouth over his. A teasing slide. "Consider yourself paid in full."

"That's not a kiss." Before she could say another word, his mouth caught hers, savored it. She grabbed hold of him, pressing close, feeling the evidence of his erection.

Despite the urgency burning through every part of her body, he seemed intent on taking his time. Slowly, he kissed her. Without any haste, he finished stripping her. Only then did he lift her and carry her into the bathing chamber. He reached for the water, never once breaking their kiss, and turned on the shower.

Since they had a moment while it heated, she took a turn stripping him, removing his shirt, her hands caressing the smooth, muscled planes of his chest. Stroking lower to the waistband of his slacks. She undid the button and shoved them down, biting her lip in hunger as his erection sprang free. Long. Thick. Hard.

Delicious.

But she wasn't allowed to nibble on it yet.

He tugged her into the shower with him, the wide head spraying them both. It felt good to sluice the grime of their trip from her skin; however, it wasn't just the heated water stroking her flesh. His fingers explored, too, traveling feather light over her curves, a light, teasing touch that ended in him cupping her full bottom.

As he pulled her tight against his frame, his rigid cock pressed against her lower belly, throbbing and ready. Just like her cleft was ready. Wet. Aching...

Still, he took his time, kissing her, squeezing her cheeks. She explored him in turn, her hands skimming over the toned muscles of his arms, down the strength of his back. She stood on tiptoe, her hard nipples rubbing against his chest, the friction so delightful.

She found herself pushed against the shower wall, but only so he could explore further. He kissed his way down the column of her neck, soft nibbles that brought delicious shivers. She caught her breath as he traveled lower, making his way to the buds that were peaked and waiting for his touch. He cupped her breasts, pushing them together, presenting them to his mouth.

When he latched his hot mouth onto an erect nub, he drew a cry from her. Her hips arched.

"Yes," she hissed, encouraging him to do more.

He sucked the tip and then nibbled again. She shuddered as she threaded her fingers through his damp hair, holding him to her breast. Not ready for him to move on even as the vee between her legs cried for attention.

He lavished her nipples with attention, sucking and biting and teasing until she gasped for breath. Only then did he drop lower. His face was level with her mound, and yet he didn't touch it. He instead kissed each thigh.

She growled. "Stop teasing me."

"So impatient."

"The end of the world is coming. We don't have time to waste."

"How true. And yet, you should be savored," he whispered, placing a kiss on her mound even as his hand slipped between her thighs. He dragged a finger across the swollen lips of her sex, parting them that he might penetrate her.

She sighed in pleasure. Arched her hips as he thrust that finger.

But it was when he placed his mouth on her that she cried out. "Tariq." His name slipped from her lips, and he made a sound against her, a rumble of pleasure that vibrated.

He lapped at her, his tongue lithe, his lips teasing. He licked her until she thought she would come. It was close. She clutched at his head, not only to hold him there but as support given her legs trembled.

Sensing her weakness, he gripped her by the hips and held her prisoner to his tongue and the pleasure it gave.

Such pleasure...

She couldn't hold on. Didn't want to. She let her climax come, felt it bursting inside, an explosion of her senses that left her gasping and throbbing, especially since he continued to suck at her clit.

Still thrust with his fingers. Kept her orgasm going.

She uttered a cry of disappointment when he stopped, only he wasn't done. He stood and grabbed hold of her leg, lifting it to wrap around his hip. He guided his cock to the entrance of her sex, and she welcomed it. Welcomed the hard thrust.

His cock filled her so perfectly. Stretching her channel. Going deep enough to touch that inner pulse that craved a hard pounding. With long strokes, he thrust, over and over, hitting her in just the right spot.

Completing her.

And as if he read her mind, his lips found hers, and he whispered, "You're mine, little queen."

His. A possessive claim that triggered her second orgasm, and in her excitement, she nipped his lip.

Nipped it hard enough to taste blood.

Not enough to feed, but enough that it exploded her senses. In that moment, she came a third time, an orgasm not of the body but...something else.

She could swear she felt him. Felt his pleasure. His

need. A link formed between them, and it was the most intense thing she'd ever experienced. So intense she hugged him close, letting it echo through her.

That closeness enveloped her in a haze that followed them from the shower to bed.

Had something special happened? She wanted to ask him, and yet, only a moment after hitting the mattress, he snored.

Seriously? She turned to look at him and saw his expression slack, his body relaxed. Sleeping.

Almost insulting except she knew how much trust it took to sleep with someone else. It helped that he reached out to grab her, hook her, and draw her back against his body. His mouth nuzzled the hair at her nape, and he whispered, "Sweet dreams, my queen."

And then they spooned.

FOURTEEN

"RISE AND SHINE, brother. It is late afternoon and time for your lazy bones to get out of bed."

Awareness took a moment. The restorative rest he'd fallen into a deep one. But at least he could say he felt much better. Refreshed.

Sated, yet hungry. His gaze darted left and right. "Where's the queen?" he asked, sitting up in one smooth motion. Casting out his senses, he quickly realized only his brother, Jamaal, was in the near vicinity.

"Your dictator is in the office the staff created for her, handing out orders and getting shit done in a way that is uncannily more efficient than our methods."

He couldn't help but smile. "She is queen for a reason."

"And are you planning to become her king?"

The sly query caught Tariq by surprise. He ignored it a moment as he noted a pile of clothes on a chair. The tags still attached. He snared the pants and drew them on to find them a perfect fit. "I see you helped her."

Jamaal snorted. "Not my doing. I woke up to find my own pile of clothes and wondered how she knew all our sizes." He pointed to his outfit: khakis, button shirt, and vest. "The steel-toe boots were a nice touch."

"I hope you were mannered enough to say thank you."

"I'm pretty sure you thanked her for all of us."

The slam of his brother against the wall knocked enough sense into Tariq to realize he held his Jamaal by the throat. On account he was angry. "Stop disrespecting the queen."

"Or else what?"

He lifted Jamaal, his hand tight on his throat. "Or else I'm going to forget you're my brother and find you a new bottle with a cap."

"You wouldn't." Jamaal's eyes narrowed. With good reason.

Threatening to imprison another djinn was the worst punishment imaginable.

"I will do it and not feel an ounce of regret. Felicia is a lady. *My lady*." Something that felt incredibly good to say aloud. "You will be respectful."

"Fine. I will show respect for her," Jamaal said grudgingly. "You're still fair game, though. Worm rider."

"Excuse me?"

"After that stunt you pulled in the ocean, I'd say you earned the name. And many more. The possibilities are endless. Memes of your holding the reins to that beast, the caption reading: Can handle any big serpent. Wrangling the mighty beast."

"Be sure to show my good side," Tariq replied as he released his brother. "Now, if you're done being jealous of my mighty worm, tell me what's happened. I assume there were no attacks while I rested."

"You mean while you snored up a storm and slept like the de—" Jamaal halted and instead said. "Slept like a baby after a bout at the tit. Not much occurred other than the queen frightening the staff. We'll be leaving at sundown."

"How long will we have to travel?" Never had he been more conscious of how he'd come to rely on the teleportation he used without thought. Forced to travel via mundane means, he understood how difficult it could be.

The good news, though? The demons appeared somewhat restricted as well. Other than the incident with Ella, they didn't just appear in places. They also had to travel, hopping bodies and quite possibly only having a short time to do so. He'd noticed there were fewer and fewer demons attacking each time.

Either some of their essences were dissipating or they were busy elsewhere. He really hoped for the former.

"The queen says we're not stopping for more than refueling, which means, at top speed, it will still take us more than a full day of driving. Probably two."

"That puts us driving in daylight. I'll have to do

something about the UV rays," he mused aloud. It would deplete the magic that hadn't yet completely restored. The power in this area appeared weak. Hopefully, he'd find some bigger pockets to siphon on their trip.

"Hold on, wannabe superhero. You don't need to do shit. Queen says the vehicles will be equipped with special windows that block the UV rays."

"Which is great until we're attacked and the windows broken." As djinn who'd once upon a time presided over wishes, he knew all about loopholes.

"Even if they're broken, they'll be fine. They'll be wearing special suits to block the sunlight."

"How many vehicles are we taking?"

"Three."

"Why that many?"

"It's safer in the sense that, if one breaks down, we can still go on as a full group." Because most vehicles could only handle five passengers, not the six they traveled with. Seven with a guide. More if the queen insisted on guards.

With the serious stuff taken care of, Tariq looked closer at his brother and noted the ragged edge of his core, but nothing leaking from it.

"How is—"

"My magic?" Jamaal held up a hand, and a golden ball of energy floated just above it. "I have some, but I'm weaker than a tadji." The baby version of a djinn.

"Give it time to heal."

"Demon wounds can't be fixed." Jamaal didn't

need to gesture to remind of the scars on the side of his face.

"Have you asked Ella if her magic can heal them?"

He shook his head. "No. And I won't until this is over. She needs her strength. We all do."

The change in Jamaal's attitude proved striking. "Look at you, sounding old and wise like our grandfather."

"Don't compare me to that crazy fool. You don't even want to hear what he thinks we should do."

Sliding on his own pair of steel-toed boots, Tariq paused. "Dare I ask?"

"He thinks we should give Ella to the demons. Says it's the right thing to do. Which, of course, sent her husband into a fit."

"I can see how it might," was Tariq's dry reply.

"To make things worse, Ella agreed. Said the ghosts were advising her to do it as well."

"Given she might be the strongest weapon we have, why would we do that?"

Jamaal shrugged. "No idea, but glad to see I'm not the only one who agrees with Zane. It's stupid. But Grandfather is insisting. Says the gods have spoken to him."

"And what does Felicia say?"

Jamaal smirked. "Queen says since we're heading to the temple anyhow, everyone should shut up."

Tariq's lips twitched. In other words, don't decide yet and wait until they got closer and knew more.

"Let's go see if Azzam has caused more trouble in your absence."

Grandfather sat moping on the opposite side of the sitting room. Zane and Ella had chosen to sit at a short breakfast bar, the witch eating to refuel her human body.

Yet, looking closer at Ella, using eyes that saw beyond the material world, he had to wonder how human. He'd only caught glimpses of her aura because of the spirits that acted as a shield around it. Hearing her speak about them, he understood she listened to a few, but did she even truly know how many actually followed her? Hundreds hovered—over, around, even underfoot, in a thick cloud—which, in turn, was an indication of the power that she could summon. So much power.

He absently mused how she compared in strength to the ancient ones that cast the demons away. Could one soul sorceress be enough?

At first glance, he didn't see Felicia. That was because she was tucked away in a corner, her back to a window with the curtains drawn, behind a large desk, three laptops running, and a phone tucked to her ear.

She saw him, arched a brow, offered a small smile, and turned away.

Brat. The gesture had him heading straight for her. He stopped at her back. Listened as she spoke.

"Are you sure they had red eyes?" She paused, and he heard the reply.

"Yes, Your Majesty. The infected human was killed, but the reports claim a mist did escape."

"And probably found another host. Keep an eye out for more. We'll be moving out shortly. Have the convoys ready to go."

She hung up, and he found himself asking, "Convoys?"

She craned to peer at him. "You didn't seriously think I'd make it easy and only have one for them to watch, did you?"

"You're splitting the enemy forces."

"I am. We can't afford to make mistakes this close to the end game."

"What's this about red eyes? Did I sleep through an attack?"

"A few tried to infiltrate the hotel. They didn't make it very far. Turns out there are ways to detect them when they've taken a host."

"How?" Tariq asked. Nothing he'd read had mentioned any spells.

"Cardamom."

"The spice?" He frowned.

"Apparently it acts like demon bane. One whiff and their eyes turn red. Abd al Jabbar, the leader of the local vampire flock, was the one to tell us about it."

"They've had experience with demons?"

"More than us, apparently. Could be the rift we're dealing with isn't the only one."

"Or there are remnants of the past incursion," he mused aloud. "After all, demons still do exist."

"In a dumber version. The ones we've encountered of late are definitely intelligent."

"Because they have a leader to guide them."

"A demon boss?" The space between her brows pinched. "So there really is a Satan?"

The remark made Tariq chuckle. "Not quite. The legions are led by super demons. Or, as the ancient texts called them, daevils. Basically, higher-ranked fiends who wield power and can actually strategize."

She mused aloud. "They act as a hive king to the drones. That's good news."

"How do you figure?"

"Simple. Remove the king and the other demons turn dumb again."

"You might be right. The issue lies in how to do so. The daevil controlling them is within the rift."

She tapped her bottom lip. "The possessed ones we've encountered haven't been impossible to beat. So I'm going to go out on a limb and say we've yet to meet the big bad."

"My research doesn't have much to say about them, other than the fact most are too powerful to inhabit a mere fleshy shell."

"Which is why the bodies sometimes explode. The big guy wants out. He just hasn't found someone who can handle him yet, which means—"

"—he is searching for a way to escape." Had the daevil found it in Ella? Tariq kept that tidbit to himself for now. "If we can block the rift, hence blocking the daevil's influence, we should be able to handle the demons that are left."

"Piece of cake," Felicia said with dry sarcasm. "How is it that you know all this? Before, you seemed to know very little about them."

"Because my knowledge was limited," he admitted. "But I've been looking."

"How? You haven't left."

"True, and my powers to conjure have been weakening." Something he hated to admit aloud, but he could no longer ignore it. He couldn't hide the fact that he might not be as capable as he'd like should it come to a battle.

"More evidence the demons are siphoning magic." She tapped a pen on the desk. "Why?"

"That's the one thing my research hasn't shown." He held up a book that he'd finally located. Not easily. In order to wish for a book, he needed to know the title. No title meant concisely worded demands. "I need a book on demons" could kill. There were millions of books in circulation on the subject. If you added the term "non-fiction," it dropped to thousands. Human scholars truly loved to write.

But he couldn't categorize by author. Or even year. Because translations might be the only existing version and they might not be as old.

It meant bribing a few scholars to do research. Those librarians and academics read through the books at their disposal and gathered the interesting tidbits, which they wrote in a journal. A magical journal that copied all text to the matching one kept in a null pocket only he could access.

Tariq waved the journal with its many notes.

"What is that?"

"The notes about the true history of demons."

Felicia's gaze narrowed. "I'm going to want to read that."

How sexy, a woman who didn't scoff at the written word. It made a male want to throw her over a shoulder and bring her back to bed.

Alas, she didn't sense the eroticism in the moment.

"Now that we're all awake, and the sun is about to set, we should get going." She stood, and he noted her outfit: tanned slacks and a long-sleeve Henley with a round neck. Small brown boots encased her feet. Yet for all that, she still had too much skin exposed. With her hair pinned atop her head, her neck remained bared, as did her face and hands.

He grabbed her by the waist rather than let her pass. "I thought you were supposed to have something for this." He brushed a knuckle over the soft skin of her cheek.

She trembled, and her lips parted. "I do. I'm just not wearing it inside."

He eyed the curtains. "Took a risk then."

"I am not walking around like a mummy in the daytime, and you can stop mollycoddling me over it."

For some reason, this made his lips twitch into a grin. How he enjoyed her strong nature. "Excuse me for caring whether or not you turn crispy."

"If things get too sunny, then you have my permission to cast a shadow over me."

"As my queen commands." He swept her a bow and, when she went past, gave her a light swat on the bottom, which she didn't even dignify with a yelp.

By the door exiting the suite, he noted a pile of cloaks, the kind that swaddled them like ghosts, one for everyone in their party.

"Not all of us are allergic to sunlight," Jamaal remarked as Felicia had them distributed.

"It's part of the plan. The guides and some random folk will be wearing some, too." All part and parcel of the plot to divert and split the demons' attention.

Everyone grabbed a bag Felicia had ordered for them because, as she remarked, "We should be prepared in case we get split up or separated from our vehicle." Each of the sacks contained different sustenance items. Food and water for Ella, more food and water for Ella in Zane's heavier pack, along with blood supplements in a pill form to pack the most nutrient punch.

As for djinn who didn't actually need food or water but existed on magic?

Jamaal held up a wand. "You sending me to wizarding school?" he asked.

"Think of it as a magical snack. I found you all some artifacts you might be able to absorb for a quicker punch."

A brilliant idea he should have thought of, but being used to absorbing magic from the very air, he'd not even thought of trying it. Tariq palmed the lighter he found in his bag. Closed his fist around it and frowned. "I don't feel any magic."

Felicia plucked it from his hand. "That's because this is just a lighter." She clicked it. A flame popped up. "To make fire."

"I can make fire," he retorted.

"With magic. But you said it yourself; it's weaker. What if you need fire and can't conjure any?"

Then he'd probably be dead.

Exiting their hotel room, they had a short walk to reach the elevator. Once crammed inside, Felicia eyed them all. "Remember the plan."

"What plan?" Tariq asked.

"We'll be splitting up and taking different vehicles. We need to lose any pursuit."

"What if all the drivers are possessed and we don't see it?" Because they'd certainly never spotted the infected pilot.

"They all have cardamom sachets to flush them."

"And if the demons are resistant to it?"

"Then we're screwed. Deal with it." She arched a brow. "Everyone remember their teams?"

Jamaal smirked as he shifted closer to Felicia, and Azzam grumbled behind Tariq. He frowned. "What teams?"

"Three groups. You're with your grandfather."

"No." He didn't pause.

"Yes. We need to be balanced strength-wise. We

can't send your brother who's still wounded with Azzam. And Zane won't leave Ella."

"Don't even bother asking," said the vampire with a dark glare his way.

"This is a bad idea," Tariq growled. Bad because he should be with Felicia. "We will have two teams, not three."

"Three is better, and you know it. Or are you saying you don't think I can defend myself?" Her chin pointed, and her stare turned icy.

He knew better than to insult her honor – and pride.

"Fine."

The doors to the elevator opened onto the main level, and he noticed a pile of luggage being shoved out the front doors heading to a line of vehicles.

"Ours," Azzam stated. Seven vehicles in total moved around.

She really had been busy. Just look at the lobby milling with groups of two dressed in identical robes, also carrying packs.

They merged into the group and split off, all moving to the front door and spilling out onto the road. Pairs piled into the different chauffeured vehicles. Except for one. Azzam climbed into the back, but Tariq went around to the driver side, opened the door, and pulled the man out, ignoring the brown eyes and spicy scent. Probably not a demon, but he didn't care. Tariq snapped his fingers, and a wad of cash appeared to placate the yelling driver.

He slid behind the wheel.

"This isn't part of the plan," Azzam declared.

"Exactly. So no one will expect it." Tariq gunned the engine and pulled out before everyone else.

"Where are we going?"

"To the rendezvous."

"But you don't know where that is. I'm the one who knows because the queen worried you'd leave me behind."

Tariq cast a glance at him. "More like you told her I would."

"We both know I won't be much help in a fight."

"Then why do you want to come along?" he asked as he cut sharply to the right down a narrow alley. He leaned on his horn rather than slow to let people saunter out of his way.

"This is the most interesting thing to happen in centuries. Did you really think I'd miss it?"

"No, but I do expect you to stay out of the way."

"I plan to. Now that we understand each other, I can give you the address."

"Don't need it."

Azzam leaned forward. "Of course you do. How else will we find the others?"

"Easy. I'm following the queen."

"How do you expect to do that when we left before them?"

"Because I know where she is." Humans had GPS; he had something a little more esoteric. Exactly how close had they gotten during sex? He'd not purposely marked her, but that didn't stop him from sensing the tendril linking them together.

Did this mean he'd somehow mated with her?

This was not the time to ponder it. This moment required vigilance. He had to keep himself and Azzam intact that he might properly throttle Felicia later for being headstrong and beautiful.

He turned left and returned them to a busier thoroughfare.

"Keep watch behind us. Let me know if you see anyone following." Because he had no intention of losing track of his queen.

"Exactly how do you want me to tell you if someone follows? People are driving all over the place." Ah yes, the chaotic nature of traffic in Casablanca. Vehicles ranged from taxis like theirs, to cars, trucks, bikes, and even mopeds. Then there were the people on the sides of the road, sometimes in it. He had to weave his way around, doing a few turns. Trusting in the tendril connecting him to Felicia, he drove them parallel to her route. He could even get a faint sense of her feelings.

Nervous, yet determined.

Determined to drive him wild. He'd lost control with her. Spending himself inside her and then leaving himself vulnerable. Dropping into a comatose-like slumber.

What did that say about him?

I trust her.

Which was a big thing for the djinn. An almost

immortal race, they nonetheless did succumb to certain things. A few rare ailments, like the pox, which they could catch from humans. They could starve their magic and kill their core. And if a djinn was in a deep sleep, a demon could simply murder them.

Usually, a djinn only slept with close family—and even that was rare—or his mate.

There was that pesky word again.

His attention veered to that thread and tested her emotion. He got one.

Irritation and then a strong thought.

Get out of my head. You're distracting me.

The emotion flung him out, and he froze in shock a second too long. Horns blared, and Azzam yelled, "Watch for the donkey."

He wrenched on the wheel and pulled over, still stunned by what had happened. Turned to ask the one male who might explain what it meant. "Is it possible to hear someone's thoughts if they're not in the vicinity?" Because while he could do it, he had to be touching the person, usually.

"Why?"

"No reason."

The cuff Azzam gave him didn't hurt but did cause him to glare. "Don't hit me."

"Then answer the question. Why would you ask about hearing thoughts unless...?" His grandfather's eyes widened. "You mated with the vampire."

"Mated?" He winced, saying it aloud. "I don't

think so. We didn't perform any ritual. We just had sex."

"Did you use protection?"

If he could have, he would have blushed at the blunt question. "No. I didn't think I had to. She's a vampire."

"So you came inside her womb?"

"This is getting kind of personal even for you."

"I'm trying to ensure I give you the correct answer. Now, did you or did you not leave your seed inside the woman?"

"Yes, but only because I know for a fact vampires can't have children."

"Not entirely true."

He blinked at his grandfather. "Excuse me?"

"Vampires can't have children with each other or humans. You aren't either. You have magic."

"And?"

"If your body wishes it, then you can impregnate her. Seed her. Make her your mate."

"I know just coming inside a woman isn't enough to create that bond. Otherwise, every young djinn who made a mistake in his exuberance would be shackled for life."

"You're right. It would require intent. If, at the moment of climax, you made a strong wish, a true one, then you might have marked her when you spilled your seed."

"How would I know for sure?"

"One clue is the hearing of your mate's thoughts."

Tariq drummed his fingers on the steering wheel.

"But that depends on the bond. The most telling sign is usually the soul string."

"The what?"

"For a djinn, you are remarkably uninformed about our mating rituals."

"When was the last time any of our kind mated?" The djinn kept to themselves, and he'd never truly cared before.

"A true mating is rare. I never found it," Azzam grumbled. "Your parents did."

Tariq didn't remember much of his own parents. According to Azzam, his father overused his magic and turned to dust. Bereft, his mother followed him.

And now, Tariq was mated to a vampire queen. Even crazier, he didn't mind it.

We belong together.

The more he repeated those words, the more he believed it. How about that? A future with Felicia. She'd probably not be happy about it. Especially when he explained djinn mated for life. But surely, she'd come around. Eventually.

Danger!

The feeling screamed at him, and yet it wasn't his emotion. It was Felicia's.

She needed him.

He slammed the truck into drive and sped away, cutting off traffic, ignoring the honks and angry yells.

"Was it something I said?" Azzam yelled.

"The demons are making a move."

FIFTEEN

UNDER THE PALE red light of the first blood moon, Ella paced the dusty road, angry, upset. Alone.

"They took him. I can't believe you let them take him." She shook a fist as she railed against the spirits agitating the air around her.

"Good riddance."

"Never liked him anyhow."

"You can do better."

The ghosts weren't smart enough to show sympathy in her time of need. They only cared about Ella's life to the exclusion of all else. And if they weren't careful, she'd show them her wrath.

It still burned hotter than bare feet on sun-baked asphalt that she'd not been able to do more. But the attack came out of nowhere. They had made it to the edge of the city and had just left the lights behind when those other cars shot out like rampaging metal bulls, clipping their vehicle and sending them careening.

The impact jolted Ella, and she hit the seat in front of her. The seatbelt she insisted on wearing—to Zane's amusement—kept her from soaring through the windshield like their driver.

Zane defied the laws of momentum, but only because he grabbed and tore loose the oh shit bar at the moment of impact.

The engine smoked—she could smell it—and she blinked her eyes, trying to adjust to the sudden dark. The attacking cars came in without lights and their own twin beacons extinguished. Her ghosts screamed around her—*"Flee the infidels." "The morality police are coming." "Time to dance with the devil in the pale moonlight."* —and she only faintly heard Zane cursing as glass continued to break.

Why are they smashing now? We're not moving.

"Stay in the car. Let me handle this," Zane ordered.

Her dark knight thrust open his door, and she saw enough to perceive the hands reaching to grab him.

Bad idea. He lunged at their attackers with a snarl, and the door slammed shut, leaving her in false safety inside the truck.

As her eyes adjusted and her brain stopped wobbling inside her skull, she tried to make sense of things. The steam rising from the hood, the gray swirl of her friends manifesting in their panic, their voices shouting all at once.

"They're coming."

"The destroyer of nations is almost here."

"I think I left the stove on."

The recent ghosts always had a litany of things they thought they'd forgotten before they died.

Her door was wrenched open and someone reached for her. They didn't get far given her seatbelt held her in. They yanked, but her butt didn't move. She fought, slapping the hands.

"Personal space."

"Don't touch us."

"Why are you letting the demons win? Control them."

The words gave her pause. Control them? Could she do that?

Curious, she let the red-eyed fiend unbuckle and pull her from the car. That cardamom spice really worked when it came to identifying the demon possessed. A pity that was all it did. Still, this was her first up close look at a possessed person. She took a moment to study the face of her captor, the rictus on it cruel. The spark in the eyes inhuman. The oily smudge on the soul kind of like a ghost.

Ella controlled ghosts. Human spirits only, until now, but she was game to try something new.

She reached for the demon essence, not with her hands but her mind. *Come here. You don't belong in that body.*

The smudge ignored her, and she frowned. Since it wouldn't obey her command, she stretched for it, again not with real hands, but esoteric versions, imagining them grabbing the demon spirit. She yanked it free. The body collapsed with a gasp.

The other people with red sparks in their eyes standing behind their companion hesitated.

They watched to see what Ella did next. She could have used a clue because she wasn't sure herself. Now that she held the demonic essence, what should she do with it?

She'd better decide quickly. It writhed in her grasp. It wriggled. Felt really wrong. She didn't like its slimy sensation at all. But how to get rid of it and make sure it didn't possess anyone else?

For once, her friends had nothing to say. They hung in a misty mass all around, watching and waiting.

A raspy, "Let it go," drew her attention to the red-eyed fiend who spoke.

"I can't." If she let it go, it would find another body. That seemed like a bad idea. She looked at the soul she held. It didn't belong here, and it offended her. Could she get rid of it? She twisted it, and compressed it between her hands, squishing it until it poofed, releasing magic that somehow bolstered her and filled the air around with sparkles of power.

"Pretty."

"Do it again."

She wiped her hands clean on her pants. Where was some hand sanitizer when you needed some? She could use a vat because she was about to get busy. She eyed the other possessed humans.

Smiled.

The red eyes recoiled.

"Who's next?" She waggled her fingers.

The demon-possessed humans tried to scatter. She caught a few and took care of their problem. One by one, those she caught were saved and their fiend destroyed.

Only as the grabbed the last one did something feel different. The eyes blazed a brighter red. The lips parted, and it hissed, "Surrender or he dies." The body exploded, and only the quick actions of her ghosts kept her from getting meat splattered.

As if she cared. The words froze her to the core. *Where is Zane?*

She glanced around and didn't see him at all. The demons he fought with were gone.

And so was he.

Where is he? she shouted inside her head to her ghostly friends.

"Taken."

"The devils have stolen him away."

"He's gone and good riddance."

The realization the demons had him broke something inside her. She let out a scream. And then another. The power she'd just accumulated welled up within.

And burst.

She wasn't too sure what happened after that.

SIXTEEN

"ELLA, YOU NEED TO STOP." Felicia pled with the woman floating a few inches off the ground, arms spread, eyes rolled back.

She'd heard the scream while driving and known it was Ella. Who else could cry loudly on a level no human could hear?

Since she knew everyone's route, and she'd expected a move on the soul sorceress, she'd kept close, but not close enough to stop the attack. She slammed to a stop behind the crashed vehicle and jumped out, ignoring Jamaal to race toward the noise of chaos erupting. She found her friend, only Ella wasn't home right now. Her ghosts were in control and having a gleefully destructive time.

Ella floated along, having turned back toward town, a tidal wave of chaos following her as awnings ripped free and undulated in the air amidst a whipping sandstorm.

It didn't go unnoticed. Lights came on. She heard the commotion of people sticking their heads out for a peek. Now was not the time for humans to get involved in their affairs.

While she might have shoved him out earlier for daring to spy, Felicia found herself wishing for Tariq's aid in extricating themselves before things got stickier.

She shouted at him with her mind. *Danger.*

Only moments after that, Tariq came to a screeching halt.

"Felicia, are you all right?" he asked, jumping from the driver's seat, ready to fight on her behalf. If the situation wasn't so dire, his response might have been cute.

She turned her dark gaze on him and said, "Ella and Zane were attacked."

"And?"

"They took Zane."

"Still don't see the problem. You seem to be unharmed."

"I am fine. As is your brother. It's Ella. She's lost control of her ghosts." She pointed to the swath of destruction and the distant sound of wood cracking and screams.

"You mean to say you only called me because your witch is having a fit over her husband being kidnapped?"

"Yes."

He glared. "I thought you were in real danger."

She smiled. "It is cute you came running."

"Not funny." He stomped off in the direction of

the screams and the crashing of masonry. "You'll owe me for this."

"I pay my debts," she retorted at his heels.

He cast a glance over his shoulder. "Azzam, watch Jamaal."

"What?" his brother yelled. "You can't be serious. I am not being babysat by an old has-been."

"Old? I can still beat you in most things."

They left the two djinn bickering and headed into the bazaar, where the stalls appeared as if a whirlwind had gone through. Curious faces peeked out from behind curtains and doors, but none dared step outside. Superstition and a healthy fear kept them in hiding.

Impressive, really. "Does Ella do this often?" he asked, taking in the destruction.

"First time that I know of. Last time, she was this pissed she took out a sorcerer trying to steal her power. He, too, made the mistake of touching Zane."

"How emasculating for him."

"Nothing wrong with a woman standing up for her husband," she huffed.

"Call me old-fashioned, but I think it should be the other way."

"Neanderthal."

"Some would call it being a gentleman."

"There's a name for guys with a hero complex who think women can't help themselves."

"Awesome."

She snickered. "That was you in bed. As a person, you're…"

"Badass. Charming. Elegant."

"Freakish. Goofy."

When he glared, she smiled. "Just keeping the alphabet theme going along. I see her." She pointed to the figure floating down the middle of the path, hair lifting and rippling in a wind that only she could feel.

Tariq strode toward her. "Ella, rein in your spirits."

That only had the effect of causing said spirits to rush the tall djinn and bear him aloft far enough and hard enough to slam him into a stall. The awning collapsed on top of him.

Felicia knew better than to try and get too close. "Ella!" she yelled. "Stop screwing around. We need to go get Zane."

The word Zane caused Ella to freeze, and she hovered midair.

"Really, I can't believe you're having a temper tantrum when Zane needs rescuing. Or do you want me to go save your husband all by myself?"

Ella pivoted, her face a blank mask, her eyes swirling pits. "We're going to save him?" Her voice emerged soft and hesitant.

"Of course we are. As if we'd let those nasty demons have him." After all, they took him on purpose. Not because they wanted Zane. It didn't take centuries of unliving to realize they were after Ella, and what better bait to dangle than the husband she adored?

"I want him back," Ella stated.

"Then let's go get him. Come on." She held out a hand, and Ella drifted to the ground, took a step. Halted. Then took another and another. Her eyes returned to normal, and she grasped Felicia's fingers in a tight clasp.

"You'll help me find him." Her voice sounded so small and lost. "I need him."

"I know you do. We'll get him back. Tariq, are you coming? We don't have time to shop."

He stood, the scarves he'd landed in tangled around his limbs. She grinned as he tossed her an annoyed glare.

In short order, they'd collected Azzam and Jamaal. She didn't argue when Tariq announced, "You and I are traveling together from now on."

Felicia also insisted they take Ella while Jamaal and Azzam took the second vehicle. The drivers were ditched.

They didn't run into any troubles the rest of their journey that night. It could have been Ella had scared the demons off, but Felicia wondered if it was more because the demons had already gotten what they wanted.

Now if only they understood why the demons wanted Ella so much.

Did this have something to do with the prophecy Zane discovered about her? Ella didn't know Zane had paid a visit to Ella's mother, only to discover the woman was no blood relation. Apparently, Ella's parents woke one day to find a basket with a baby nestled within. Whoever had left her also provided documents attesting they were the parents, plus a sum of money. But the strangest thing was the cryptic note. "Guard her well, for the fate of humanity may rest on her."

Was this the moment the note spoke of? Would Ella save the world?

Only one way to find out. Packed with gas cans, a few supplies, and not much else, the pair of Land Rovers left the city and its suburbs. Tariq took the lead. Jamaal and Azzam followed, their bouncing beams illuminating the darkness outside.

Felicia sat in the passenger seat beside Tariq. Ella had the back, where she conversed with ghosts rather than the living. She sat in the backseat, nodding her head and occasionally staring off into the distance.

Tariq flicked his glance to the rearview mirror a few times before he mentioned it to Felicia. "I don't know if it's a good thing she's talking to ghosts."

"They can be a great source of information."

"If she stays in control."

"Have faith. Ella's stronger than you think."

"She laid waste to a marketplace because she was upset."

"Could have been worse. Given they took Zane, she could have decimated the city."

"She's dangerous." He said it knowing full well Ella could hear him.

Felicia frowned. "No worse than you or me."

"She's not doing it for her own self-preservation."

"You mean you've never done something for someone else?"

"Have you?" he countered.

"Yes. Not often. And maybe not so dramatically, but then again, I've never been that much in love."

"Ever?" For some reason, he sounded angry.

Even odder, she felt his anger...and hurt.

Why hurt?

She glanced at him. "Love is a weakness. Love makes you lose control." She cast a glance back at Ella, who no longer appeared to be communing with anyone and stared blankly out the window at the dark shapes flashing by.

"Love is supposed to be the most powerful thing of all."

"Maybe it is." For some reason, she couldn't help but glance at his side profile, the hawkish nose, the firm line of his jaw covered with a soft burr. "Have you ever been in love?"

"No. Yes. Maybe."

"That's not a clear answer."

"Because love is complicated."

On that they could both agree.

But it didn't help the strange stilted chasm between them, one comprised of things unsaid. How did someone say, thanks for last night, can we do it again?

Could their relationship go anywhere? A djinn and a vampire. It sounded impossible.

Not impossible.

She cast him a sharp glance, only to find him staring straight ahead.

Rather than pummel him for possibly listening in and replying, she placed a hand on his thigh. Nothing more.

Just a hand.

He placed his atop it.

And thus did they travel. The chasm between them partially breached. The words unspoken, but an understanding beginning to form.

When the first purple edges of dawn crested, she didn't argue when he declared they'd stop for a rest. She felt the fatigue pulling at him.

Ella didn't. She sat up and grumbled, "Why are we stopping?"

"We need to take a break."

"No, we need to catch up to Zane."

"It won't be long," Felicia reassured, yanking on her gear. Goggles, hood, gloves. The latest in vampire daytime wear. "He just needs to fuel up and stuff. You should get out and stretch your legs."

Instead, Ella paced.

Tariq filled the gas tanks, and Felicia stuck close to him. "She's a mess. I'm worried about her when we do reach the rift."

"Will she turn against us to save her mate?"

"Yes." She didn't hesitate to reply. "Zane is everything to her."

"We cannot afford for sentimentality to get in the way." Tariq's statement emerged flat.

"What are you saying?"

"I'm saying we need be careful lest our strongest ally be turned against us."

The worst thing was, Felicia didn't disagree. The life of one wasn't worth the fate of the world. But Ella would never see it that way.

As Tariq emptied the can and then checked the oil and other things on the truck, Felicia sat in the shade, weary and worried.

She'd known Zane a long time. Could she sacrifice him if events demanded it?

She closed her eyes. *I don't want to find out.*

SEVENTEEN

"SHE'S GONE," he heard Felicia exclaim, followed by cursing.

Then his brother grumbling. "Why are you kicking me?"

"You were sleeping." Felicia's terse remark had Tariq blinking the sleep from his eyes. He rubbed his face, fighting the lethargy.

When had he fallen asleep? He didn't remember them planning for that. Last he recalled, he gassed the truck. A truck he currently slept under. He rolled out and popped to his feet in time to hear his brother ask, "I don't remember us stopping to camp."

"Because we didn't," Tariq claimed. "Our sleep wasn't a natural one." He'd never even seen the spell cast on them. Which made him wonder how the soul sorceress even did magic. Did she not require words or gestures, or could she do things merely by thinking it?

Whatever the case, the ghosts did her bidding.

While his magic weakened the further they drove, Ella had only gotten stronger as more and more ghosts flocked to her.

"Dammit, Ella. Why did you have to go and do that?" His queen sounded exasperated.

Despite having stopped early in the day, twilight now prevailed, the sky still pink and orange in the distance. Soon they'd see the moon. Would it be red again?

"Where did she go?" he asked.

"To find Zane, of course," Felicia retorted.

"Wasn't that exactly what we were doing?" He scrubbed a hand through his hair.

"I guess she overheard our conversation and took offense. She also took the other truck."

As if being put to sleep wasn't bad enough, she'd stolen from right under their noses. How embarrassing.

"How long has she been gone?" he asked. The lingering slumber evaporated as the problem unfolded.

"Hours," Felicia spat. "I doubt it took her long to dump our asses out. She gave herself a huge head start."

"That was foolish." He checked on the truck as Azzam stuck his head out of the window and peered around with one eye.

"I should have seen it coming," she grumbled.

Jamaal wandered off and frowned at Tariq. "Why are you doing things the hard way?" The hard way being Tariq using his hands to lift the hood and check the fluids. "Don't tell me you can't feel it." Feel the lack of magic in the area. While Tariq's magic had mostly recovered, he had none to spare, and there was none to be found. For some reason, the farther they traveled, and the closer they got to their destination, the less magic there was available for him to feed on. As if something had sucked it dry. What he did manage to find felt weaker.

"Why again are we doing this?" Jamaal complained as Tariq indicated he get into the back of the vehicle.

"Because," Tariq remarked.

"We're not heroes."

"Nope."

"We're barreling into danger."

"Yes." Tariq didn't disagree.

"We'll never catch her in time. We're way behind," his brother noted.

"The third blood moon isn't until tomorrow night." Felicia indicated the asteroid in the sky, its hue more pink than red still.

"Great, still time for us all to see the world ending," Jamaal offered with sarcasm.

"Or in time to stop it." Tariq wasn't about to add his pessimism to his brother's.

"Stop it how? Because we both know your queen won't allow us to kill Zane, and if they're holding him hostage, then we won't be able to rein in Ella."

"Ella's a smart woman. She'll do the right thing." He hoped. The life of one wasn't worth the fate of the world. His gaze strayed to Felicia, and his forehead creased.

Is one life worth everything?

Depended on the life.

"Are we leaving yet?" Azzam asked, once again sticking his head out the window. Was it Tariq, or did his hair seem a little darker than before? His magical core a little thicker?

"In good time. In case you hadn't noticed, we suffered the loss of a party member."

His grandfather waved a hand and announced, "The witch acts as the gods command."

"By going off on her own with no support or plan?"

"Who says she doesn't have a plan?" Felicia remarked, clambering into the passenger seat, leaving the driving to Tariq for the first leg.

"Problem is her plan might end up opening a door that lets in a legion of demons. Excuse us if we'd rather not all die," Jamaal retorted.

"Are you always so pessimistic?" Felicia countered. "Ella isn't some helpless little sorceress."

"How about rather than arguing, we put our energy to how we're going to fight the demons and close that rift?"

"I vote we stuff Azzam in the hole," Jamaal volunteered. Which led to another round of bickering, the lighter, teasing kind.

It didn't last, though. Tariq drove as fast as he dared over the rough terrain. Unfortunately, despite being real close to the source of their problem, they'd yet to come up with a solid plan. Mostly because they didn't know what to expect or what to do.

Azzam proved little help, other than saying the gods would reveal the solution when the time was right.

Hastening the answer with hands around his grandfather's neck only got Jamaal a glare from Felicia that had him releasing Azzam and sulking in a corner.

The queen might not possess magic, and yet she oozed a power that influenced.

The moon remained a glaring reminder that they were running out of time. They needed to do something before it rose for the third time. How could they stop whatever the demons planned?

Why hadn't they brought more allies? Sure, Tariq had no kin to call upon, and yet the vampires could have helped. Tariq and the queen could have also contacted the other races. Asked them for aid. Yet, here they were, alone on a hard-packed dirt trail, moving cross country, hopefully going in the right direction.

Two broken djinn, a mighty queen, and a confused male. Against a legion.

The question spilled from his lips. "Are we suicidal?"

Felicia snorted. "Excuse me? Where is that coming from?"

"Why are we facing the demons without any backup?"

"Because there wasn't time to find anyone," she stated.

"You had ample time to arrange transportation and

supplies. Surely you could have hired some soldiers," he prodded.

"I could have, but..." Felicia paused. "How would they have helped us? Humans would be susceptible to the demonic possession. Even vampires are not immune. I, for one, preferred to not ride with strangers who might kill us when our backs are turned. And, really, how would more people have helped?"

"It is how the gods wished it." Azzam's pronouncement was met with stares. He shrugged. "All mighty quests are undertaken by the few."

"These few have the fate of the world in their less-than-many hands," Tariq retorted.

"Then don't fuck up." Jamaal snickered. "Boy, is everyone screwed if we're supposed to be the heroes in this tale."

"There wasn't really time to gather an army," Felicia said, chewing at her lower lip.

"There would have been if we'd not wasted so much time traveling to you in the first place. But someone didn't mention we had a time limit." Tariq's gaze in the rearview mirror focused on his grandfather.

"Just doing as told. According to the gods, we are exactly where we should be."

"Which isn't reassuring at all," Tariq growled.

"What's that?" Felicia leaned forward, and the argument was dropped.

As he slowed down, his headlights caught what she'd seen. The other truck, abandoned, the driver door hanging open. He stopped, and Felicia jumped out, making haste to check over the vehicle. He joined her. While she sniffed for blood, he spread his hands and looked for signs of lingering magic.

Nothing. Not a single trace of Ella. But on a positive note, no blood either.

In grim silence, they clambered back into their own truck and the trek resumed.

Maybe fifteen minutes or so before dawn, Tariq slammed to a stop by a copse of sad-looking trees. "We should stop and rest."

"I don't think any of us are feeling fatigued. We need to keep moving," Felicia declared.

"The sun will rise soon," he observed, having watched the growing hints of purple on the horizon.

"So I'll swaddle." She pulled out her gear and layered it on.

"We don't need to rush. We're only a few hours away at this point, and this might be our last chance for shade. The third moon is not until tonight. We have time."

Felicia shook her head. "No, we don't. Call it a premonition, but we need to be there. The sooner, the better." She placed her hand on his. "I appreciate the concern, but..." Her voice lowered. "Either you move this truck, or I'm going to go vampire squirrel on your neck and drive for you."

"Vampire squirrel?" he queried, putting the vehicle back in motion.

"It's an expression Ella coined. Zane lets her watch way too many bad vampire movies."

"Are there any good ones?" he asked.

"A few."

"Then once we've saved the world, you'll have to watch them with me."

In the back seat, Jamaal gagged. "Seriously. You did not just say that. Hundreds of years old and that's the best you could do?"

Tariq's lips flattened. Felicia's hand came to rest on his thigh and squeezed. "It's a date."

A date they'd keep, which meant getting them to that abyss and finishing this once and for all.

He drove even faster than the day before, stopping only to unstrap cans from the top of the truck and fill the tank. He didn't care how much gas he wasted. He'd worry about that later. First, he needed to ensure they had a tomorrow.

The edge of the abyss loomed suddenly. A black crevice out of nowhere. Tariq only barely managed to brake. The truck shuddered as it continued to slide. It slowed as the gaping maw of the chasm loomed. There might have been a few sighs of relief as they stopped. Then a single gasp as the front wheels dropped over the edge, giving them a jolt.

"I think we found it," Jamaal remarked.

"I think I need new robes," Azzam muttered.

Sitting in the open, Tariq was more aware of the sun than ever. It was mid-morning, and it shone bright. Felicia might have covered herself as best she could, but he could feel how the rays taxed her. Just like being here taxed him.

The very air sucked at Tariq's magic. Absorbing it. Stealing...

If it affected him, who was whole and strong, then how much worse for his damaged grandfather and brother? A glance at Azzam showed him sweating and Jamaal not far behind him. Their wounded cores had begun to seep again.

Not good. What could they truly do to help? Nothing.

"Time for the pair of you to leave," Tariq announced.

"We are not abandoning you to be a martyr," Jamaal snapped.

"This magical suck is going to kill you." Tariq waved around at the air. "You're no good to me dead."

"He's right. We can't have you two slowing us down." Felicia exited the truck with a hiss. "Why did it have to be the desert? Why not a lovely underground cavern system with lakes and pretty rocks?"

Jamaal went to follow her, but Tariq had already engaged the locks and then used the driver control to prevent Jamaal from changing it.

If his brother wouldn't see reason, then he'd force the issue. Tariq stepped out of the truck and then expended some magic. Enough to yank it from the edge of the cliff. He jammed the door locks, given his brother had jumped into the driver's seat. Sticking it in second gear, Tariq placed a magical rock on the gas peddle, forcing it to drive away. Jamaal would eventually wrestle control, but by then, hopefully, he'd see reason.

Felicia was already out of sight, having dropped below the crevice's edge, moving quickly to avoid the sun. Looking at the long, winding path that hugged the rocky wall, he wanted to sigh. He'd already used as much magic as he dared. A djinn walking. He never thought he'd see the day. Meanwhile, Felicia ran as best she could, her shape a dark moving shadow against the reddish sandstone. He quickened his own pace to catch her.

When she paused in the shade of a shallow cavern, he joined her and asked, "Are you okay? Do you need me to create a shadow umbrella for you?"

She shook her head. "Save your magic. I'll be fine. I just needed a little break because it was getting hot. I'm ready to go again."

"Last one to the bottom gets head."

She snorted. "You do realize, with that kind of incentive, I might just shove you off the path."

He grinned. "Or we could tie and both lose."

"Now you're talking."

He grabbed her gloved hand, and they began to run down the steep path, barely more than a single file track that, at times, was not even a few inches wide.

But they didn't slow or falter, not when the deeper they went, the less the sun's rays fought to singe her skin. They made no attempt to hide. He wasn't sure if anyone would detect him using magic, and she was right. Save his strength.

No one sounded an alarm. As a matter of fact, they saw and heard nothing at all, yet he knew they were in the right place.

He could feel it. A certainty humming in his core.

He might not believe in the same gods as Azzam, but he understood the weight of portent. The shadows thickened, and it was dark enough at the bottom that Felicia pushed up her glasses and perched them atop her head.

"That's better," she said with a sigh. Felicia didn't stand around enjoying it. She set off at a brisk pace, and he took long strides to keep up with his queen, who was fearless and ready for action.

It made her so sexy.

It wasn't long before they made it to the edges of a camp: a half-dozen tents, crates, a few ATVs covered in camouflage netting. The signs of habitation meant Tariq held himself ready to fight.

Placing a hand on his arm, Felicia shook her head. "There's no one here. No one alive."

Since he could feel a touch of her hunger through their link, he didn't question her statement. Much like he could sense magic for nourishment, she knew how to find food. They took a step between the first pair of tents. The door flap on one was pulled back, and he could see inside. A pair of messy bunkbed cots. An open chest with clothing spilling out of it. On the other side, the flap hung down. He kept going, warily watching the abandoned camp, the only sound that of a loose flap rustling with a breeze. Other than that, there was no movement. Not even a hint of smoke from a cookfire. Only as they passed the second set of tents did it occur to him.

There is no breeze.

That was when the monster attacked.

EIGHTEEN

IT CAME OUT OF NOWHERE, lunging with a yodeled meow. Its claws sank into Tariq's thigh, and he yelled.

"Argh. Demon!"

Whereupon, Felicia laughed. "It's just a cat."

He glared at her. "Just a cat says the woman who doesn't currently have all millions of its claws sunk into her skin." He turned his stern gaze on the feline, a kitten really, which decided to climb the rest of him and wrap herself around his neck. The little thing shivered.

"Get if off me," he said through gritted teeth.

"It's just a poor, scared kitten." Only as the words emerged from her mouth did she grasp what she'd said. Scared of what?

The shadow gave her just enough warning to dive to the side. She hit the dusty ground hard and immediately pushed herself up. She spun and blinked at the monster.

"What is it?" It had the body and mane of a lion, yet despite the muzzle and sharp snarl, its features held a human cast. A ridge of spines went up its back, and its segmented tail possessed a barbed tip like a scorpion.

"Manticore," Tariq grimly announced. "Don't let it sting you. It's poisonous."

It was also stalking them, its shaggy head following Tariq's slow movements.

"Distract it," she said.

"I might not be able to do much." He didn't say it, but she heard it somehow. *My magic is so weak.*

Then it was up to her to save him.

The manticore lunged, Tariq yelled—mostly because the small kitten chose to launch itself, using its claws to find purchase to spring.

As her djinn lover dodged out of the way, Felicia darted closer. She grabbed hold of the manticore's mane, the fur of it silken and fluffy. It would make a lovely coat.

The mighty beast let out a roar and shook its head. But she held on.

"Beware the tail!" Tariq shouted.

She whirled and narrowly missed being impaled. Before the deadly stinger could try again, Tariq was there, gripping it with two hands, muscles bulging.

"Kill it," he hollered.

"If you insist." Since a mouthful of fur wasn't a good time for anyone, she had to rely on her nails. She drew on her vampire self, the one she kept under control most times. The tips of her fingers elongated and sharpened, enough she could rake them across the manticore's neck.

It slumped to the ground, and Felicia licked the tips of her clawed fingers. "Gamey," she said with a grimace.

"Says you. I say it makes a nice snack," was Tariq's reply. He had his head back and inhaled.

"Are you eating it?" she asked with a wrinkled nose. She eyed it and made a moue.

"It doesn't have the greatest magic, but it has some. No point in wasting it."

"Think there's more of them?" she asked, looking at the other tents with suspicion.

"Doubtful," Tariq said, peeking into another tent and emerging with a machete.

A strange and rough noise started. She turned to see the kitten had returned and rubbed against Tariq's ankle while purring.

"Looks like you made a friend."

"I've never had a pet before," he said. He appeared confused as he stared down at the little creature.

"They're like a girlfriend. Just remember not to come home smelling like another pussy." She winked as she sashayed past him.

"Just so you know, I am a one-pussy kind of djinn."

"You'd better be." It didn't take a crystal ball to see he was hinting he wanted something more.

She wouldn't mind that.

But first, they had to find the temple of doom. The one in Ella's vision. Funny how Felicia began to recognize the place from that short video montage they watched. The slit in the rock, the tunnel with its muffled sound effects. The fear they'd arrived too late.

Tariq was right. Why did they come alone? How could she have been so stupid as to not see someone manipulated them? She never left home without a cadre of bodyguards. Or a packed lunch. She'd not brought anyone from her circle other than Ella and Zane, who were already part of the quest.

Tariq at her back was the only solid thing right now. But could she trust him to protect her? The djinn were known to be selfish. He'd shown himself different thus far; however, this would be a true test of his character.

Of hers as well.

Did the world really deserve the ultimate sacrifice of her life? What of Zane's?

She'd better decide soon because the tunnel lost some of its murkiness as it widened onto a chamber filled with light. She hugged the wall to peek, noting the brackets studded around the cavern held torches that burned brightly. Could she blame them for the pulsing heat bathing her skin and penetrating even deeper than that?

Tariq paused beside her. He whispered, "I think we found the place."

"Was it the stone temple that gave it away?" she

muttered in reply. Seeing it via the screen replaying the memories and experiencing it in person were two different things.

How to explain the awe of being in the presence of something ancient and huge? The relic towered, the stonework an intricate work of skill and art. A thing of beauty...and chock-full of power.

She felt it, like a hum in the air that emanated from the rock wall framed in numerous etched stone pillars. She could almost see the magic in the glyphs, as if they glowed. Perhaps they did because the unsightly crack marring the wall certainly held some color. The fissure outlined and glowing in red. For Hell. Blood. Death.

The later two she didn't mind. Nothing wrong with a bloody death if it fed a need. However, this was her world, not Hell's, and she was damned if she would stand aside to let it take over.

From the crack oozed an ochre mist, the tendrils moving without a breeze. She didn't need Ella's power to guess what the vermillion fog meant. Swirling demonic spirits looking for hosts. Bad news, but not what truly drew her attention.

Sitting cross-legged on the ground before that giant crack? The missing Ella. And she didn't look happy at all.

NINETEEN

"TRUSSED up like a turkey about to get roasted."

"Free yourself. Or don't. Hehehehe."

The voices offered all kinds of advice as Ella sat on the ground, legs folded lotus style, her hands tied behind her back. As if mere rope could hold her. But she let her captors think her subdued. Played the meek and subservient prisoner. She'd do anything they wanted until she set eyes on Zane.

Because she was here to save him—even if he'd grumble that he was supposed to save her. Thing was he didn't seem to understand that his love saved her every day. It kept her from going too far. From letting the ghosts take control permanently.

Without him, I would be lost.

"Not lost. We'd be there for you."

Exactly what she didn't want, which was why she had to get him back. Oh, and save the world, according to the new ghosts hovering all around chattering at her.

By now, she should clarify that she meant just met because, when it came to age, these were the oldest spirits she'd ever encountered. And boy did they have lots to say once they realized what Ella was.

"You mustn't wait until the blood moon. That is when the rift is strongest. It will be harder to seal shut."

"Be sure to use every spirit you can find."

"Even the living."

The last piece of advice caused her to cast her glance at the people who'd brought her here. They lined the walls of the cavern, slack-jawed and red-eyed. Definitely in need of a priest and some holy water. Given the creepy vibe they exuded, she kept expecting them to suddenly crack a few new joints and spider climb the wall to dangle on the ceiling.

For the moment, they didn't move or speak. Did nothing but stare and drool, which might be a good thing given there were more of them than expected. Ella and the gang had assumed the demons sent all their guys out looking for them. Wrong. Apparently, hunting Ella and friends down was only part of their plan. The other part involved the piles of merchandise scattered before the temple.

The giant cavern was filled with stuff. Magical stuff. Gorgeous glass bottles, the jeweled exteriors wound with intricate workings of gold and silver. Given the bulbous stoppers on them, and the fact they occasionally rattled despite no one touching them, she'd wager they housed the captured djinn. They weren't the only things collected. Vases and armor, jewelry and wands. There was a mishmash of items stacked in piles, with one thing in common.

Power.

Lots of power.

The kind needed—along with the blood moon only hours from rising—to crack open a door and invite in the legions of darkness.

A few of her ghosts actually wanted that to happen.

"All hail the dark days."

"It is the time for the prince of thorns to rule."

"I wanna be a minion of evil."

However, Ella wasn't a person who thought she would thrive in a world of only shadows and fear. Sure, Zane might enjoy not having to hide during the daytime; however, even he would have a problem with the loss of his fancy wardrobe and fast cars. Demons weren't into the whole industrial revolution thing. Destruction and death were their jam, not the capitalists' dream.

Apart from her need for strawberries picked fresh from a field, the sun needed to remain because Ella enjoyed the feel of sunshine on her face. Less so demon claws ripping out her heart. That would hurt.

But how to stop it? She'd come here hoping to find out. Lucky her, there were spirits she could ask.

Eyes shut, she rocked in time to the buzzing words of the ghosts swirling around. So many of them these days. Hard sometimes to tell them apart. But she had to sift through them, shutting out the ones who spoke

English, looking for the melodic tones of the old ones trapped here for centuries. Their spirits bound into the stone of this place. Twelve, to be exact. The thirteenth one had escaped, and if she didn't do something, the other twelve would follow and the world would end.

As to how one managed to get away? The genie who'd spilled his blood on the stone was how. His death released the first spirit lock.

The head devil had hoped to find twelve more, but the demons sent on a mission to acquire miscalculated. They killed before counting.

It cost them. Only eight bottles lined the step. Apparently, genies were a little scarcer than expected. There weren't enough to break the spell, which was why there were still twelve locks. The devil didn't want to waste the djinn he had. In order to put them to best use, he set a trap.

For a soul sorceress. Because only one with control of the spirits could amplify the magic.

"The devil wants you, Ella," the voice cackled.

So he stole Zane to force her to do his bidding.

She stopped breathing as she discerned her husband nearby. His anger a dark, seething thing.

He sensed her. Knew she was near. There existed such a strong bond between them. He'd told her, "You are the only thing that makes me feel alive." She was his reason for being. Through their link, his love pulsed strongly, as did his determination to protect her at all costs, even the price of his own life.

My dark knight. Didn't he understand dying wasn't

acceptable? Good thing she'd arrived and would make sure he didn't foolishly pay it.

Showtime. She only had to ask her spirit friends, *Free me,* for them to snap the ties binding her. Foolish devil. Did he really think he could control her? She'd come to Hell's rift willingly. She *wanted* to be here.

Ella stood, hands by her sides, calm inside despite the danger. She had to be steady. Ready to act. She saw the red pinprick eyes all focused on her.

Good. Had they heard what happened to their friends? She'd be more than happy to give them a first hand re-enactment.

Before she could reach and squeeze the closest one, she froze.

Froze because Zane suddenly appeared, trussed tight in a cocoon of silk webbing and dangled by a...

Long.

Hairy.

Jointed.

Leg.

"Spider!" Yeah, she didn't keep that scream to herself. How could she? This went beyond eight-legged freak into nightmare.

Like any person doing her best not to pee herself in fear, she stared as the monster of nightmares lowered its bulbous body on its sticky rope, taunting, with a swinging Zane–whose dark eyes glared at her.

She could read the message. *What are you doing here?*

Ella waggled her fingers in reply. "Hey, honey. Missed you."

Would those words count later when he punished her for putting herself in danger? Hopefully not. She did so like it when he got overprotective. He usually made her scream—in pleasure—for hours.

He angry-talked with his gaze some more. *Get out of here.*

As if she'd leave. Zane was here. Even though her biggest fear had come to life, she wouldn't run. Maybe wet her panties a little, but she would stand against the arachnid minion of evil. She just hoped it didn't have siblings. She dared a peek overhead to see if she could spot another amidst the jagged stalactites dangling from the ceiling. There were too many shadowy pockets, so she sent some of her ghosts to find out. A few others went to check on Zane. Her beautiful husband. About to become spider food unless she acted.

Ella planted her hands on her hips and made her demand. "Put him down. Right now, or else."

She didn't really expect a reply, yet she got one. The very crack in the wall itself seethed and breathed, the words deep and resonating, understandable, if chilling.

"Open the door and you can have your mate."

"If I open the door, you'll eat me and my mate."

"If you don't, he dies right now." The silken thread holding him shortened, and he was drawn to the mouth of the arachnid. A big mouth. With teeth.

"Think he'll scream when my pet bites?"

Being the manly stoic type, probably not, but Ella would.

"Open the door."

She couldn't ignore the voice. Heard its command.

Didn't dare disobey, not with those shearing mandibles so close to Zane's head. Even she couldn't fix a decapitation.

But...*I don't want to end the world.*

World or Zane?

In the end, there was no real question.

TWENTY

THE GRATING VOICE wasn't meant for Felicia or Tariq. Yet they heard it. Heard the awful choice that was almost as bad as the monster that would enforce it.

The dilemma was clear. Ella would open the door to save Zane, which meant they had to act.

Of course, Tariq had his own solution. "We need to force the spider to kill the vampire."

"How does that help?" she snapped.

"It puts Ella into a rage, and she'll do anything but help the demons."

Felicia glared. "Or how about we save Zane, make her super happy, and then she saves the world from annihilation."

"Your way sounds harder."

"My way doesn't have her hunting us down afterward and tearing our souls out to torture us for our role in her husband's death."

"Harder it is." Tariq eyed the spider, Zane, the

wall. Then pulled a knife and threw it. In the battle of wills, with thick magic and spirits choking the air, no one noticed the metal blade. Yet it sliced through the cord holding Zane. He dropped hard.

Ella gasped. "Zane!"

"Get out of here, moonbeam!" he yelled. "Don't let them use you."

At his words, all hell broke loose. Not literally. The crack was still just a crack and not a doorway, but the minions against the walls sprang to life. Although with their red eyes, snarls, and jerky movements, they seemed more undead.

Possession didn't agree with them.

They loped toward Ella, slack-jawed and fingers extended like claws.

Some might see a horde of trouble. Felicia's tummy rumbled. "You take care of the spider that wants to eat Zane. I'll handle these," she said, dropping into a crouch.

"There's too many," Tariq argued.

She snorted. "Not for me. You might be weak against them, but you forget they're in human bodies. Also known as a buffet." She didn't worry about what he'd think if he saw her tearing into flesh. Either he accepted what she was, or he didn't. Best to find out now.

Ignoring Tariq, she rushed the demon-possessed humans, cutting them off before they reached Ella. The first one stretched to grab her, and she allowed it, only to regret it as a second later as she felt the adrenalized strength.

This wouldn't be as easy as usual. But she didn't mind a challenge.

She also didn't fight nice. A kick to the balls hurt the possessed just as much as a regular guy. When he doubled down, she grabbed his head and wrenched. He dropped, and she had two pairs of grasping hands to contend with.

She was lucky they didn't choose to attack with weapons. Actually, there was little finesse at all. She absently wondered, as she tore into a jugular, if the longer a demon possessed, the less able a body became.

Grabbing hold of another, she swung him and noticed from the corner of her eye that Tariq had made it to the temple and faced off against the spider.

Better him than her.

Where was a giant can of Raid when you needed one?

TWENTY-ONE

IF ONLY THE cartoon-sized cans of bug spray really existed. He would have expended all his magic to call one to battle the eight-legged freak he faced. However, Tariq had almost no magic left. The rift in the stone sucked at it. He only had himself. His wits. His need to prevail. Oh, and the thought that if the world ended, he'd never get to be with Felicia. He really wanted to be with her. So he'd better ensure it happened.

He drew the machete he'd managed to keep and used it to slice at the leg that jabbed at him. The blade stuck in the hairy appendage and ripped away.

Not exactly the most propitious of events, but it gave him a moment. He dropped to his knees and used what magic he had left to burn at the silken strands binding Zane.

They turned to ash, just in time. The vampire rolled and missed the leg that stabbed down with a pointed tip. Zane scrambled to his feet.

"Can you conjure something to kill it?" Zane asked.

Tariq shook his head and then danced, his back arching, his hips drawing inward as another leg swung. "I used the last of my magic to free you." Better give it to an ally than feed the hungry rift.

"Any ideas?" Zane ducked and rolled, coming up under the spider. A punch upward didn't even make the thing flinch.

Only now did Tariq wish he'd searched the camp for better weapons. He'd relied so long on his magic he didn't often think to equip himself. Good thing someone had gotten used to living within his means and not magic.

Crack. Crack.

The gunfire echoed loudly in the space. The first shot missed wildly and hit the wall in a shower of sparks. The next rounds, though, hit the spider in the head. It shuddered and recoiled. The third, it let out an unearthly squeal as part of its eye exploded in chunks. And still Jamaal fired.

His damned fool of a brother, refusing to obey and leave.

Thank the gods.

With the arachnid retreating, Tariq focused on the room. Azzam had chosen to aid Felicia, who—while looking slightly battered and bloody—grinned at him.

The fact she had time to breathe could have indicated she'd vanquished the possessed humans. But it didn't. Rather, they'd turned their attention to something else. The bottles.

"Oh fuck." The expletive slipped from his lips as the first minion grabbed an emerald-colored glass and flung it to smash on the wall. The screaming mist that emerged was sucked right into the rift.

Good-bye, Balthazar.

A new fissure appeared, and they all heard the pleased and resonant chuckle from the other side.

Tariq ran for the rest of the bottles, not fast enough to stop the ruby red container from getting shattered. Or the amber decanter.

He had no magic to protect his people. But he had to stop it. Stop them from being killed. Thus, he attacked with his bare hands. His virtually human hands against the demon-infused bodies. He felt them trying to claw at his core, his empty magical core.

He grinned. "Nothing there, suckers."

The bottles stopped smashing as his allies joined him in ridding the world of the bodies that hosted the demons. With nothing else close by, the demons returned to a misty state, and he began to believe they'd win.

That perhaps they might walk away alive.

Then Ella spoke. Only Ella wasn't home.

TWENTY-TWO

"TOO LATE, puny creatures. Already the wall breaks, and now, with the help of this witch, it shall be destroyed." The words hissed from Ella's lips as the devil leader used her to speak. However, she drew the line when he attempted to add in an evil laugh.

Only Ella could muahahahha. She grabbed hold of the devil's piggybacking spirit and held it tight.

It wiggled in her grip.

"Let me go."

Only she could hear him, hear the astonishment as she clenched his incorporeal form.

Why would I let you go when I need you to fill in a crack?

It didn't take a genius to see how the spell keeping the rift sealed worked. Sacrificed souls locked the magic in place. More souls also unlocked it.

The mistake Azzam and the rest made was they

assumed the mention of the thirteen who'd originally put the spell in place was they were all sorceresses.

Wrong.

Then, as now, there was only ever one soul sorceress.

And thirteen djinn.

Those genies gave their magical lives to seal the hole. They willingly bound their spirits to the wall holding back Hell. Prisoners for all time.

Until an idiot tried accidentally set them free. The powerful dying blood of a djinn cracked the spell and freed one of the trapped spirits.

Which gave Ella an idea, and it involved the demon spirits. The key word being spirits.

Had everyone forgotten what she controlled? The devil had thought to use her to remove the djinn souls powering the spell. And she would, but only so she could replace them.

Keeping a grip on the strong soul of the devil, she reached up and plucked a floating demonic mist. It wiggled, a tiny little bug in the scheme of things. She yanked it along much as a mother would yank the ear of her child to get it to behave. She slapped it against a crack, still stained in the blood of the djinn who died and started the chain reaction.

The devil in her grip stilled. Whispered. *You don't want to do that.*

Actually, the very fact he appeared fearful was why she did.

The demon mist wiggled in the crack, sought to

escape, but Ella slapped her hand on it and *pushed*. Not exactly the right word and yet the only thing to explain how she ground it into the crevice and cemented it there. The spirit screeched as it found itself caught. A cry cut off as a tiny section of the fissure pulled together.

She heard her allies whispering. "What is she doing?"

Fixing the wall. What did it look like? But she fixed it better than her earlier counterpart. Rather than sacrifice anyone, she used demon spirits to power the spell, using the bigger ones for the largest parts of the cracks. Once she got down to the hairline ones, she had to get fancier because those fine filigrees still had djinn spirits holding them together. She swapped those souls with demonic mists, letting the sigh of relief from the released spirits fill her with strength. Because now that the trapped djinn were ghosts, they could help her too.

Still caught in her grip, the spirit belonging to the devil struggled. It understood its fate.

"I can make you powerful."

Hello, she was already pretty awesome.

"Let me go and I'll return to my side."

Too late. This monster had threatened her husband. That deserved punishment.

Only a tiny hole remained in the wall. A red, glaring eye.

The devil fought, twisting and cursing, doing his best to escape her firm esoteric grip. When he couldn't break free, he heated his mist self to boiling temperatures and scalded her ghostly hands. It hurt, but she gritted her teeth and bore the pain. Letting the devil go wasn't an option.

Marching to the wall, she stood on tiptoe and shoved the legion leader in it. Did she feel bad she turned him into a fancy lock against Hell for eternity? Not really. He shouldn't have touched Zane.

Turning away from the now pristine temple, she clapped her hands and beamed. "All done."

"Seriously?" Tariq glanced at her then the wall then her again. "That's all it took?"

"It was harder than it looked." She lied to show modesty. "I don't know about you all, but I could go for an ice cream sundae." Instead, she got a Zane-wich. He wrapped her tight enough in his arms a few joints cracked. But she didn't break.

She wasn't that fragile, not anymore. However, when he planted a kiss on her... Her knees buckled.

Good thing he held her up to shake her. "You idiot! What were you thinking coming after me?"

Ella blinked. "Of course I did. I love you."

"Crazy," he said with a shake of his head. "What am I going to do with you?"

Her lips curved into a teasing smile. "Find us a tent and I have some ideas."

Apparently, he had a few of his own.

TWENTY-THREE

THE DANGER WAS OVER, and the adrenaline began to wane. It was then Tariq truly realized they were all alive. The world was saved, and while he'd only played a minor role in the end, he'd done something.

While Zane carried off his giggling wife, he made his way to Felicia, only to have to hold himself back from kissing her given Azzam stood there.

"Did you see me? I haven't boxed like that in centuries." His grandfather, who looked more like an uncle now with his sleek dark hair, beamed.

Jamaal looked just as smug. "Doesn't need me, my brother says. Good thing I arrived when I did, or you'd be spider shit."

"Perhaps I was hasty in refusing your help," Tariq admitted.

"Hasty, he says. I was a hero." Jamaal couldn't help but grin even as wonderment colored his words.

"So was Tariq. That was quick thinking what you did with the spider silk holding Zane." A disheveled Felicia praised him, and he basked in it.

"I'm just happy my practice paid off. I spent almost an entire century honing my knife-throwing skills."

"It took you a century?" Her lips quirked. "I learned in a year."

"Showoff." He smiled at her and hugged her close.

She allowed it, but he could feel her tense as she eyed the pristine wall. "Is it really over?"

"Can't you feel it?" He held up his hand, and a ball of pure magic formed in it. "The chasm to Hell is closed once again, and magic is returning." In large part because the piles of treasure on the floor were losing potency as Tariq's starved djinn core sucked at it. He didn't feel bad at ruining the ancient relics. Most of the stuff would have been useless anyhow with how the rift tainted it. Still, he'd bet the Templars wouldn't be pleased to lose their chalice, and he'd wager there would be many who would not be happy the Philosopher's Stone was once more just a rock.

Felicia left his side to inspect the remaining bottles, the one thing he couldn't drain. "I'm sorry we couldn't save all of them. Is this really all that's left of your people?"

Five bottles. He sighed. "Could be there are a few more scattered around, but we were never copious to start with." He grabbed the corks that stoppered them. Opened them and yet nothing came out.

Felicia frowned. "Are they dead?"

"No. They probably haven't grasped how close they came to dying."

"Don't they realize you're the last of your kind?"

"They don't care. Which is why I'm going to leave them here."

"Here?" Her eyes widened. "But what if someone finds them?"

"Then perhaps they'll manage to shake them out of their complacency. Might do us some good to grant a few wishes and become a part of the world again."

"Speaking of the world... I don't know about you, but I've had enough of dusty caverns and tents. What do you say we hop into a truck and find a town with a shower and a bed?"

"Drive?" He shook his head. "I know something faster. I'll see you both later. Much later." He waggled his fingers to his brother and Azzam before drawing her close.

"What are you doing?"

"Magic, my little queen. Your wish is my command." He kissed her and, with a twist of magic, moved them somewhere else.

She drew away from him and exclaimed, "You found me a bathroom?" She laughed and looked around the large and lavish room with its stone floors, massive tub, and even bigger shower. "I love it. But what about everyone else?"

His first impulse? Who cared? Except, she did care, and he kind of did as well. "Our companions are fine. I'll return later to give your witch and her husband a way back home." As for Jamaal and Azzam, he'd seen signs of their cores recovering, which meant they could take care of themselves. "Why are you so worried about them? You should be worried about me."

"You? What's wrong with you?"

"It's been too long since you've been naked in my arms." He leered and waggled a brow.

She smirked. "Is that so?"

"And, according to you, I did technically save the day."

"I guess you deserve some kind of reward." She tugged at her blouse, popping the buttons of her shirt.

Too long. He snapped his fingers, and her garments were gone, leaving her deliciously bare.

When he reached for her, she laughed and danced out of his grasp. "Not until I shower."

As if the water would make her clean. He joined her, and despite his use of soap all over her body, it was a dirty pleasure. He stroked and lathered every inch of her skin.

Then she retaliated, her hand gripping him firmly, tugging and pulling until he gasped.

"I don't suppose there's a bed nearby," she whispered against the lobe of his ear.

In a blink they lay upon fresh sheets, and he pressed his mouth to hers, a fierce kiss to match the energy coursing through him. Touching her was like putting his hand in the hottest of flames, but rather than pain, it was excruciating pleasure.

The kiss evolved from a fierce assault to gentle

exploration. Her fingers clutched at his shoulders, the tips digging into his skin as she sought to draw him closer to her. He understood the need. He reveled in the feel of her soft body cushioning his.

With his heavier body covering hers, the hard length of his cock was trapped between them, throbbing against her lower belly. Their mouths were meshed with the occasional clash of their teeth, accompanied by their hot pants.

Her legs parted, and he settled between them, the tip of his cock nudging the entrance of her sex.

But his queen wasn't one to be meek.

Rather than ask, she used her strength against him, flipping him onto his back and straddling him. A goddess with her hair dangling down her back, her breasts pert and tempting. Her lips curved in a smile that showed her pointed teeth.

"Going to bite me?"

"Can I?" she asked.

He bared his throat. "You can have anything." His blood. His heart. His soul.

However, she ignored the invitation to slide down the length of his body.

"What are you doing?"

"I owe you something for saving us from the plane wreck."

His mouth rounded as he realized what she intended to do.

Her fingertips skimmed down his torso until they reached the prize. Two prizes. One hand gripped his heavy sac, kneading him, while the other grabbed hold of his shaft.

Anticipation had him sucking in a breath, closing his eyes, and tilting his head back.

He didn't see but rather felt when she leaned forward, the ends of her hair brushing his skin as her mouth latched onto the tip of his shaft. She gave him a little suck, but it was the nibble that caused his hips to buck.

She held on and kept teasing, bathing his cock with her tongue. She licked from his fat head down the edged rib of his shaft then back up again. She swirled her tongue and then chomped with sharp teeth. He cried out.

Not in pain, even if she punctured skin. It was pure ecstasy as she took him into her mouth and sucked. Sucked him hard enough to draw blood and have him bucking again.

He could hear her thoughts, unfiltered and raw. *Taste so good. Love this. Love him.*

Love.

The moment he realized it, his own feelings swelled and met with hers. Her turn to shudder, and through their bond, he felt her need. She needed him.

With a final lick over the head, she released his shaft and straddled him. The swollen tip of his cock poked at her damp sex. She teased him some more.

However, he was done with that. His hands clamped around her waist and pushed her down. They both cried out.

This was how it should be. The two of them joined. Him moving deep inside her. Her hands, braced on his chest, nails digging into his skin. Her head went back as she rode him, and he stared at her, fascinated by the sight of her taking her pleasure.

Impaled on his cock, he helped her to rock back and forth, grinding deeply into her. Loving the bliss, loving her.

Their rhythm took on a feverish pace.

So close. The thought hit him, and he flipped her onto her back and drove into her, pounding into her flesh, over and over until it hit.

A climax so powerful it wrung a cry from him and left her with her mouth open in a soundless scream. But in his soul...he heard it.

Love. You.

To which he replied. *Love you, forever.* And wished they would always be happy before he spilled inside her.

Spent, he collapsed beside her but kept touching her. Stroking her skin. Amazed he'd found her after centuries of being alone.

As they lay curled around each other, she asked, "This bed is huge. Where are we?"

"My bottle."

"What?" she shrieked, almost putting a crack in it. "How do we get out?"

He grinned. "I know a genie you can rub."

EPILOGUE

WEEKS LATER...WITH the world never realizing how close they came to being demon fodder.

Appearing as pompous as always—making her own butler jealous—Hendricks entered the dining room bearing a rather large tray. Without saying a word, he set the large silver chalice in front of his mistress.

"Oooh, dessert," Ella crooned. "I am so telling Zane to give you a raise."

Felicia eyed the giant bowl of ice cream in front of Ella. And not just ice cream—banana, caramel sauce, peanuts, and some marshmallow fluff, too. The girl devoured the huge mound as if it were nothing. Then again, she was eating for two.

Whereas Felicia...she sneezed. Again.

Ella giggled. "Bless you."

Felicia glared. At least she tried to while also doing her best to ignore the sparkles in the air.

"You sneezed magic again," Ella remarked.

"This is Tariq's fault." No one had ever warned her that a djinn could impregnate a vampire. Because the damned man had mated with her.

Which she couldn't get mad about because she'd kind of decided she wanted to keep him, too.

After she got over being annoyed he didn't ask.

Even the baby was a good thing, especially knowing it would automatically take after its daddy. So no blood-sucking toddler, just a mischievous tadji, as Jamaal kept teasing. They'd already begun the search for a special nanny.

"How are the cats doing?" Felicia asked. Because Zane had no choice but to cave when Azzam decided to reward Ella for fixing his magic. Matching tiger cubs. It made the kitten Tariq adopted seem tame in comparison.

"Cats are good, although we might need a new bed. They used ours as a scratching post."

"Tariq's cat smells." Damned thing liked to wake her by sitting on her chest and releasing gas. Tariq claimed his research showed it was a sign of affection. Felicia knew what it was. A power play by a pussy. Which was why she'd begun hinting to Tariq about getting a dog.

Ella licked her spoon and eyed her empty bowl with downturned lips. "I wish I could have more."

"Then have another."

"No time."

"What do you mean no time?"

A commotion on the street drew her attention, and

she peeked out the dining room window to see the streetlights extinguishing one by one.

"They're here," Ella sang.

"Who?"

"My parents."

"I thought they were dead."

"My real ones," Ella announced as her eyes took on a glow. "Don't tell Zane and be ready."

"Ready for what?"

"We might have to run for our lives."

THE END?

I don't know. I honestly never expected to write a second book after Crazy, then Even Crazier came along. So who knows? Craziest could be in the future...after all...Ella hasn't had those babies yet. And poor Jamaal, can a woman ever love a scarred and sarcastic Djinn?

Looking for more giggles?

www.ingramcontent.com/pod-product-compliance
Ingram Content Group UK Ltd.
Pitfield, Milton Keynes, MK11 3LW, UK
UKHW042002230426
12048UKWH00009B/483